Poppy shouted at Belle who was now beside her in the other seat. "Hang on, honey. We're bustin' out of here!" She eased into reverse, backed slowly until she felt a light bump, getting all the running room she could for their forward thrust through the closed garage door.

In the side mirrors she saw a shower of sparks fall from the garage ceiling and land smoking on the steps that led from the garage into the house. The garage suddenly filled with dense smoke. The headlights were like two white shafts attached to the front grill.

Time to go!

Now!

She dropped the transmission into low, eased down on the accelerator, braking with the other foot.

Off the brake!

GO!

The tires whizzed, squealing against the cement floor, then grabbed and they shot forward, a Toyota juggernaut aimed at freedom.

MURDER AT RED ROOK RANCH

BY
DOROTHY TELL

A POPPY DILLWORTH MYSTERY

The Naiad Press, Inc.
1990

Printed in the United States of America

Edited by Ann Klauda

Cover design by Pat Tong and Bonnie Liss
   (Phoenix Graphics)
Typeset by Sandi Stancil

Library of Congress Cataloging-in-Publication Data

Tell, Dorothy, 1939—
   Murder at Red Rook Ranch / by Dorothy Tell.
      p.   cm.
   ISBN 0-941483-80-0
   I. Title.
PS3570.E518M87   1990
813'.54--dc20
                                                              90-6130
                                                                 CIP

For Ruth — light of my life —
lover, partner, friend —
forever.

About the Author

Dorothy Tell lives and writes in Texas with Ruth, her lover of seventeen years. She enjoys writing, fishing, wood sculpture, and reading lesbian fiction. She looks forward to retirement (in five years) from her "day job," when she plans to write full time.

BOOKS BY DOROTHY TELL

*Scheduled for publication in 1991.

SPECIAL THANKS:

To the women of Naiad Press — my heroes.

To Ann Klauda, my editor, who with her dedicated care and attention has made the editing process fun.

To Katherine Forrest, my senior editor, who continues to give me writing help and encouragement.

To all the members of my writing/critique group — whose support continues to be as necessary as air.

And THANK YOU to the BOOKSELLERS — those hardworking people who make it possible for this lesbian author to reach her readers.

Author's Note

This novel is a work of fiction. It is set in an imaginary Texas county on the Red River due north of Dallas. Some place names are genuine, but this is only a device to add authenticity to fictitious characters and events. In this novel the people and the settings exist only in the imagination of the writer and her readers. Any resemblance to fact is coincidental.

TABLE OF CONTENTS

PROLOGUE
Big Girls Don't Cry

Nan Hightower drove the supercab Chevy pickup steadily up the rocky road to the top of a bluff that overlooked the river far below. The double sets of rear wheels whizzed where a slash of morning sun had melted a patch of frost. Nan braked impatiently as the knobby tires grabbed and pulled evenly again.

She turned the dooley off the road, rolling slowly through the golden frost-tipped grass and stopped just short of the steep drop-off that offered an

1

unobstructed view from one of her favorite places. No one was there waiting on her. Habitual earliness had stood her in good stead once again — she would have the advantage when the meeting began.

The need to walk and exercise her stiff legs pulled Nan from the comfort of the plush cab. Ordinarily she'd have ridden Beauregard, her favorite stallion, but last night's long walk and unaccustomed climb had knotted her muscles and stiffened her knees. Hell — it wouldn't do to give in like this very often — but the summons had been urgent and there wasn't time to call Zoe and have the General saddled up. The truck's heavy door closed behind her with a satisfying, made-in-America clunk.

Nan straightened her back and leaned away from the gleaming side of the truck. She curled both strong hands into tight fists, flexed, then fisted again, loving the stretchy-tight feeling of the fine glove leather molded against her knuckles. She stretched her arms up into the sparkling air of a perfect Texas autumn morning, then turned her head both ways to loosen tired muscles. She sniffed the sleeve of her black riding jacket, drawing in the pleasantly erotic odor of expensive new leather.

The smell reminded her of Morgana and brought back the pain of yesterday's devastating discovery. She shrugged off a wave of enervating despair that threatened to wet her cheeks with tears she thought she'd left behind in girlhood.

The truck's powerful engine clicked and pinged as it cooled, sending petroleum vapors into the air. Nan gazed down across the bright yellow tops of the cottonwood trees that marked the winding path of the river. Her clear blue eyes caught the spiraling drift of

2

a hawk and she idly watched it until it dropped below the line of the smokey horizon, where Oklahoma's green shoulder met the sky a hundred miles away. The popping sound of a nearby pumpjack made her smile as always when she thought of the oil it pumped from the ground and into the big Texaco refinery that turned it into dollars that flowed back into her bank account.

She stood on the bluff, legs apart, hands on hips, surveying her realm. The Hightower spread, Red Rook Ranch. Six thousand acres of prime Texas, almost surrounded by a great circling pink-silver loop of the Red River.

A movement on the rock ledge just below caught her eye. A dark figure emerged from the early morning shadows.

"What th'! Where th' hell did you come from?"

"That doesn't matter. We have to talk." The voice was low, muffled behind a gloved hand.

"Well, c'mon up here, then, where I can hear you."

Nan braced her foot, leaned forward to grasp the open hand stretched upward for assistance, and placed her head in exactly the right position to receive a forty-five caliber lead slug with an X etched deeply into its nose. It entered her left temple and exited just below and behind her right ear, taking with it not only the last cognizant thought of a woman who would never know what hit her, but also a large amount of bone and brain and a brand new amethyst earring.

– 1 –

Pushing Buttons

Poppy Dillworth efficiently guided the Toyota Chinook R.V. onto the rain-slick shoulder of Texas Farm Road Star 12. She glanced impatiently at the hand-drawn map Marcie thrust toward her.

"Well, hold on a minute, Ladybug. Wait till I get this thing off the road," Poppy said as she set the brake, removed her glasses from their perch atop her head and adjusted them on her nose so she could see the small writing.

"These damned trifocals are gonna be the death of me yet." She yanked them off and rubbed vigorously at each lens with the lapel of her blue flannel shirt, as if she could polish away sixty years' worth of corneal changes by cleaning the glass she looked through. "There now." She jammed the glasses back on her nose and squinted at the yellow tablet paper.

"Well, here's the problem, child." She flicked the paper with a thickened thumbnail and looked over her spectacles at her young friend. "You had the thing upside down. That N there is for north."

Marcie poked at the tear that threatened to trail down her plump cheek. "Maps oughta have U for up and D for down. 'Specially if you're going west. I'd have to sit sideways to get it right." The tear got loose and was joined by another as Marcie warmed to her complaint. "And anyway — you didn't have to yell at me like that."

Poppy struggled as impatience battled with remorse for primary emotion of the moment. As usual, the sight of Marcie's tears gave remorse the needed edge and she slid her bony fingers over Marcie's fleshy hand and patted it.

"I really didn't yell, Marcie. Be fair now. I just barked a little. And really — don't you think a detective course *should* have a section on map-reading? That's a pretty rudimentary prerequisite to finding things — wouldn't you say?" She smiled at Marcie and squeezed her hand, hoping she had softened the effect of her earlier behavior.

Marcie sniffed and grinned back. "Yeah — I guess you're right. It's just that I get so worked up wanting to do my best, Poppy. After all — this is our first real case. It's not just homework or a game.

This is for real and I don't want to make any mistakes."

Poppy sighed inwardly at the truth in her partner's concerns. She herself probably wouldn't have been so irascible if she wasn't feeling some of the same pressure. She'd spent forty years waiting before she retired as a clerk in the Caliche County Sheriff's Office — waiting, wanting, but never allowed to help in the investigations. This was different. Now the show was all hers.

She smoothed out the map her friend Zoe had sent and fixed in her mind the number and direction of turns necessary to bring them to the big wrought iron gates of Red Rook Ranch, where Zoe was ranch manager for the Hightower operation. Poppy swung the sleek little R.V. back onto the road. They traveled the next few miles in thoughtful silence, past fields dotted with fat white Charolais cattle.

Marcie was right. This was their first real opportunity to test their skills as private investigators. And it promised to be a doozy. Nan Hightower's death had been ruled a suicide by the local sheriff's department, and Zoe Zentmeyer disbelieved that enough to hire Poppy and her partner to prove the ruling false. Poppy had known Zoe for fifteen years and her money was on Zoe. But what a puzzler. Poppy's mind wrangled with the few details Zoe had given over the phone. Not enough yet to go on — she would just have to wait until Zoe could fill them in on the whole picture. Poppy looked forward to spending the next few days with her old friend, "catching up" on the last few years, as well as solving the puzzle of Nan Hightower's death.

Right on target, just after they topped a steep hill, the ornate gates rose, silhouetted black against the gray clouds of the early December sky. A red castle tower, or rook, the Hightower brand, reflected from the center of each gate.

"Wow," Marcie offered, her voice low and awestruck. "Sure says money, doesn't it?"

Poppy grunted agreement as they rolled to a stop. She opened her door, stepped from the cab and stretched. She marched in place a few seconds, unconsciously keeping time with the tap-squeak of the wipers to make sure all her physical systems said *go* after the long drive from Dallas. Just the usual pain in knees and hips and stiff back and shoulders.

"Don't ever get old," she said over her shoulder to Marcie as she moved toward the voice box on a nearby post. "It's the pits."

She glared at the instructions printed beside a row of buttons, grabbed her glasses from their usual place atop her head, plopped them on her nose and looked again.

"Damn," she grumbled as she angrily clawed them off and rubbed them free of the drizzle that fell softly around them.

Nope, Ladybug. Don't ever get old. Cause no damn thing works any more. Nothing — zero — nada —

"Please announce yourself." A female voice, tinged with the unmistakable androgynous authority that said lesbian big-girl, boomed out of the louvered speaker on the pole.

Rattled, Poppy interrupted her glasses routine,

straightened her spine and growled, "Miz P.A. Dillworth and partner, Marcie Judy. Come to see Zoe Zentmeyer."

"Push the red button and hold it down while you speak," instructed the dyke in the box.

Poppy felt her face redden as she cleared her throat, pushed the proper button and repeated her terse announcement.

"Yes — you are expected." The voice lightened as though its owner was smiling, then continued. "When the gates open, just drive through and on up to the compound. Zoe's cabin is around behind the main house — take the fork to the right. I'll call Zoe and tell her you're here. The gate will shut and lock automatically once you're inside."

"Thank you," Poppy barked at the box, but it had a dead sound as if no one was there any more. She released the button and returned to the dry warmth of the truck cab. The imposing gates swung silently inward on oiled hinges, fully revealing a well-tended, paved ranch road in much better condition than the state road they had just left.

A huge galloping black horse emerged from a clump of green cedars, thundered to a mud-splattering stop beside the fence and hung its head over the top rail, breathing puffs of steam at Poppy's side of the R.V.

Poppy glanced at Marcie, whose brown eyes had widened apprehensively, and said, "Well, better suck it up, Sugarpie — here we go."

* * * * *

9

A fire-spent oak log broke with a snap into three bright pieces as Zoe placed new wood on the fire. Poppy watched with admiration as the tall slender woman deftly one-handed the scoop and pushed the glowing embers back under the fire dogs.

Poppy darted a quick look at her partner whose expression hadn't changed much since their arrival at the gate an hour or so earlier. Marcie's eyes now followed with avid interest the movements of Zoe's long capable fingers as she replaced the tools and adjusted the screen between them and the cozy fire. Marcie's round cheeks glowed with higher color than usual and Poppy thought it probably wasn't caused solely by the glow from the fireplace. She'd forgotten Zoe's preference for plump women. And, from the way Zoe kept adjusting her tooled leather belt and running her thumbs and forefingers down the creases in her Levis, evidently she hadn't changed her predilection.

Poppy cleared her throat and tapped a yellow pencil sharply against the edge of her little three-ring notebook.

Zoe hastened her attention back to Poppy and her face sobered from the wide grin she'd been flashing at Marcie. She ran a work-hardened hand through her thick white-blonde hair and sat on the edge of a hard bench across from Poppy and Marcie. Mostly Marcie. Poppy still thought Zoe would look more at home in wooden shoes than western boots. She reminded Poppy of the blue-eyed Dutch boy on the paint can label.

"OK, Poppy." Zoe acknowledged Poppy's rapping bid for attention. "I know you got a million questions — so fire away."

"Actually — I'd like to get your story of what happened on tape."

Marcie dug into her shoulder bag and produced a voice-actuated tape recorder no bigger than her shirt pocket. She handed it to Poppy.

"Uh, well . . . yeah. Okay." Zoe's already low voice dipped a notch. Poppy noted with a suppressed chuckle the incongruity of this hundred-and-forty-pound woman, who could easily control a thousand-pound horse, seeming so self-conscious and clumsy in the presence of technology.

"Where, uh . . . where do I start?"

"Just start talking about what you know about Nan's death."

Zoe stood again and hooked her thumbs in her belt loops, jamming her fingers into her jeans pockets. "I get so damn mad when I start thinking about how those idiots in town screwed everything up." She paced in front of the fire. "If Bubba'd been here it'd been different. He's the only one in the department that's got any sense."

"Bubba?"

"Bubba Swindell — Sheriff Swindell's son. He's a deputy. But he and Red, his wife, were in Denver that week. I think he was as pissed off as me when he got back and saw how bad the whole investigation was botched up."

Zoe stopped her pacing and raised both hands, palms up. "I mean — Nan wouldn't have committed *suicide*! And even if she *did* — she would never have done it that way. No note? Way up there on the bluff away from the house? She wasn't even *dressed* for it — for crissakes!"

11

Zoe had loosened up and her voice grew stronger as she forgot about the little red-eyed recorder on the table beside her. "No, the whole thing just doesn't make sense. I don't care if they *did* find powder burns on her glove and that old pistol *did* used to belong to her daddy. Somebody murdered her and made it look like suicide. Somebody damn smart."

Marcie raised her hand like a child wanting permission to speak, then jerked it back and stuck out her chin in response to Poppy's frown.

Smooth move, Wondercrone. Ten to one she cries again. Poppy's inner voice supplied castigation for her impatient disapproval.

"I'm sorry, Marcie," Poppy lied. "I was concentrating too hard. Did you have a question?"

Marcie pulled her chin back in and spoke to Zoe. "Well. I was wondering who you think that somebody is? I mean, do you have any suspicions about who murdered your boss?"

Zoe stood in front of Marcie again. Her thumbs again found her favorite belt loops as she answered. "I've got this one idea that keeps bothering me, but everyone around here looks at me like I've lost my mind when I say anything about it."

"Everyone?" Poppy asked.

"Well. Violet Cooper for one. And Lupe for another. But, that's enough. They're the women who count around here since Nan's g-gone." Zoe's voice faltered and she worked her throat for a second at the evident pain of remembering Nan's loss. Zoe sat suddenly and put her hands to her face.

Poppy waited quietly for her friend to regain composure, but Marcie acted from what Poppy was beginning to realize was a deep well of concern and love for anyone in pain or trouble. She took one of Zoe's big rangy hands in both of her smaller ones and patted it.

"You must've loved her a lot," Marcie said softly.

Zoe looked up at Marcie with gratitude and spoke, her voice full of emotion. "Yeah. You're right, I did. And Nan wasn't an easy person to care about. But she treated me more than fair in the nine years I've worked here. And I *miss* her. She was more than just my boss. She was my friend. Ya know?"

Marcie moved across the empty space between them and sat beside Zoe, one soft, comforting arm across Zoe's shoulders. Zoe snuggled close and, Poppy thought, made optimum use of Marcie's bent for rescuing strays.

Well that's what you get, Dillworth. You coulda told Zoe that Marcie was straight. But that probably wouldn't've made any difference, would it? Probably be a lie before long anyway. C'mon, be the bad guy and break this up — we got crooks to catch. Our reputation's on the line here.

"Harumph." Poppy followed the directions of her inner prompter. "Well, who're these two women you mentioned and what's this idea that's been pestering you?"

Zoe jumped to her feet and Marcie sat very still and glared at Poppy. Her face glowed deep red with embarrassment as the implications of Poppy's pointed *harumph* came home to rest.

Zoe flexed her jaw muscles and looked down at her boots. "Sorry, Poppy. Guess I wandered a little there. Lupe Montalba is the cook at the ranch house but really she's sort of Nan's old *abuela*, uh, grandmother. She came to work for the Hightowers

13

before Nan was born. In fact, she's just pretty much part of the family up at the big house."

Zoe drew in a breath, seeming on the verge of many more kind words about Lupe, but Poppy gently cut her off.

"Is Ms. Cooper the financial manager you told me — us — about on the phone?"

"Oh. Yeah. Violet. She's the boss now, but actually the ranch is running itself. I mean — I'm running the livestock and land end of it. I guess she's handling all the administrative stuff with the gaugers and the oil companies. I've been trying to talk to her for the last few days about the plans Nan had started for Morgana's organic beef supply operation. But Violet's been holed up in her movie room since Nan . . . since the . . ."

"Whoa up — who's Morgana?" Poppy asked.

"Oh, you're gonna love her. Morgana the Greedy. I've never heard a last name. She's one of those California lesbian-feminist, let's-all-live-in-a-commune, witchy-woman dykes, and she turned Nan's brain to mush about six months ago. I can't stand her, but I don't think she killed Nan. She had more to gain if Nan was alive."

Zoe paused and looked at the fire, a thoughtful expression on her face. "At least — I guess she did. We'll all find out more about that on Friday when they read the will." She looked back at Poppy. "And that brings me round to the idea that's been afire in my brain about who might have done it. It does seem a little far-fetched, 'specially since no one around here owns up to having heard from him since he split for Canada to dodge the Vietnam draft."

She paused again and socked a fist against her open hand for emphasis. "Junior — J.C. Junior, Nan's no-good brother — that's who *I* think did it!"

– 2 –

Appearances

A cold front had moved through during the night, pushing the rain and clouds toward the Texas gulf. The morning sparkled. An enormous bowl of blue sky cupped the earth from horizon to far horizon.

Dark, curving archways accented the startlingly white walls of the ranch compound's main hacienda. The whole rambling house was solidly roofed by red

Spanish tiles that seemed to change in the sunlight from burnt orange to deep carmine as Poppy walked up the path from Zoe's cabin.

She looked back as voices caught her attention. Marcie stepped, laughing, from the doorway of Zoe's cabin and followed Zoe up the walk toward the picnic area where Poppy stood.

Yeppers. Looks like all kinds of changes in the air this morning.

Poppy turned her observations back to the large ranch house and grounds. Steam rose from a long, heated pool at the immediate rear of the house, where someone swam with efficient strokes, barely splashing. Poppy watched with interest as an old woman walked toward the pool from the cabana and held out a robe for the shapely swimmer who emerged, otter-like, from the flashing water. The robe was so pink it hurt Poppy's eyes. The swimmer extracted ear plugs, popped her head on either side with the heel of her hand, and hugged the woman who'd brought the robe. She then walked quickly through the cool morning air and disappeared into the house.

The old woman scanned the area nervously and spied Poppy standing by the closed beach umbrella. Her hand flew to her mouth and she whirled away, following the trail of wet footprints into the house.

Zoe stepped up beside Poppy. "That was Lupe. We must've just missed Violet's daily dip."

"Not if Violet swims like Esther Williams, looks like Claudette Colbert and wears clothes a drag queen'd kill for."

"That's Violet all right," Zoe affirmed. "Did you meet her?"

"Well, no, I didn't meet her. I've been standing here by this bumbershoot like a cigar store Indian waiting for you and Marcie to get your morning giggles out of the way."

They both looked down the path at Marcie who'd stopped to inspect a collection of colorful pots filled with cactus and plants with blade-shaped leaves. She bent close to one and the sun outlined her generously molded behind, echoing the sensuous shape of the *ollas*. Zoe's face showed her appreciation as she turned to Poppy and said softly, "Pops — you old fart. If I didn't know better, I'd say you were jealous."

"Humph." Poppy snapped her head around. "I guess I do seem a little prickly — but you're right, you do know me and I'm not jealous. I guess I feel more than a little proprietary when it comes to Marcie. She sorta helped me find my way out of the woods this past summer and I feel like I owe her, you know. Kind of protective, like a parent, see."

"Yeah, I see. And I'm the big ole, bad ole butch she needs protection from, right?"

"Well hell, Zoe. She's *straight*. I just don't want her to get hurt, that's all. She was all set to be a missionary down in South America before we met on that trek up to the mountains. And now she's studying real hard to be a detective."

Zoe watched with obvious pleasure as Marcie turned and pointed her ample bosom in their direction.

"Okay, Pops — I understand — but I got to tell you, she's the sweetest and roundest and best-looking little ex-missionary/detective I ever saw. And if she's straight I'm the Queen Mother.''

"Well, I didn't say she wasn't leaning a little.''

A stabbing memory of Irma and how it used to be hit Poppy's chest like a fist. God — she missed her — going on five years now, and still the pain could almost cut off her breath. Irma would've known exactly what to tell Zoe. But Irma was dead, and Poppy grabbed her memories by the bootstraps and yanked herself back to the present morning's quest.

Marcie joined them as Poppy turned toward the house and said, "Let's get on up there and see if Ms. Cooper will give us an audience. I want to talk to her and Lupe before we go examine the scene of the crime.''

Poppy looked back at Zoe as they single-filed up the narrow steps past the pool. "D'you think it's dry enough to get up on the bluff today?''

"Oh yeah. The jeep'll get us just about anywhere we need to go. I've given Rick and the rest of the hands their instructions, so I'm free to do whatever you think is necessary, for as long as it takes.''

Zoe pressed a button by the back door which was opened quickly by the woman who had attended the swimmer. So rapidly, in fact, that Poppy got the idea she'd been standing just inside watching them.

Zoe took command of the introductions. "Lupe, *Abuelacita,* these are my good friends from Dallas, Poppy Dillworth and Marcie Judy. They're partners in a detective agency. I've hired them to look into the matter of Nan's death.''

Lupe raised her bushy white eyebrows, then brought them quickly together in a wrinkled frown. Her carbon-black eyes blazed suspicion as she asked

19

in a clipped, barely accented voice, "Does my lady Violet know about this?"

"No, Lupe. Not yet. I was going to tell her, but you know how she's been. She ignores my messages and stays in that black hole of a movie room. I'm hoping, *Abuela,* that you will tell her we're here and that we *must* speak to her."

Lupe rubbed her hands on the hem of her apron in what Poppy surmised was a nervous habit, as her hands appeared to be dry and clean. "Well, I suppose it is okay. I think something should be done about the terrible lie the sheriff has reported about *mi querida.*" Her black eyes glistened with emotion. "But, you know that Miss Violet does not agree that you should be stirring things up about that? That she believes the report of suicide to be true?"

"Yes, Lupe, but we must talk to her anyway. Please try to get her to see us for a few minutes."

Lupe appeared to consider Zoe's request for a moment and then her white head dipped in consent as she reached a decision. "All right. Yes — I will ask her. I will tell her we must have a meeting like Miss Nancy used to have when we all needed to know about ranch business. And that is true. I have decided to leave the ranch and go to my people's home in the Valley. I am too old for all this loco stuff going on and I am frightened to stay here. So Miss Violet will have to arrange for a new housekeeper."

Zoe's mouth fell open in surprise as Lupe turned decisively and left the room without another word.

"What did she mean? Loco stuff going on?" Marcie asked.

Still looking a little stunned by Lupe's

announcement, Zoe answered. "Uh, stuff . . . well, she probably means Morgana. Lupe took an immediate dislike to Morgana. She resented her influence over Nan and mistrusts her motives."

A speaker over the door crackled slightly. *"Please bring your friends into my sitting room."*

Poppy recognized the voice as belonging to yesterday's dyke in the box. They followed Zoe through a sunny atrium that surrounded a square pool with edges tiled in turquoise, black and white. Green water plants moved slightly as big orangey-gold fish fanned them aside in their haste to present open mouths for the sprinkle of food that fell from Lupe's hand.

The women entered a large room furnished with sumptuous, hanging brocade tied back with tasseled ropes. The center of the white tile floor was covered with a thick, expensive-looking oriental carpet. Brass bowls and jars accented every corner. Poppy's eyes drank in the richness of design and texture that so differed from the airy southwest style of the rest of the house.

Well, well, perfect atmosphere for us private eyes, huh Dillworth! Ali Baba and the Forty Thieves got to be around here somewhere.

Poppy eyed with alarm the cushions scattered about the floor. Her knees were still complaining about the drive from Dallas. She thankfully noted a grouping of conventional chairs by the far wall. She wandered around looking at paintings, trying to identify the slightly spicy, aromatic scent that pervaded the room. Something between sandalwood and cedar.

A soft, tinkling sound came from a hallway off to

21

their left. A dramatically beautiful woman swept into their midst on a cloud of white satin and ostrich feathers.

Yep. That's either Violet Cooper doing the Thirties or Claudette Colbert doing Jean Harlow as a brunette.

"Hullo," the woman said, Tallulah style, and turned to Zoe. "Dahling, forgive me, I haven't been . . . myself."

Poppy choked back a guffaw. She pressed her fingers hard on her Eve's apple and fought with the comedienne in her head. *I know — I know goddammit — it's the straight line of the century, but we gotta suck it up here, girl. Get ahold!*

Violet Cooper smoothly Bette Davis'd a cigarette into a long pearl and silver holder, waved back the ostrich plumes that fingered the air about her neck and executed an Oscar-winning Joan Crawford snap-glow-suck-blow as she lit her cigarette with a heavy serpentine table lighter.

Poppy snapped to as a burning sensation clued her that Marcie had just pinched the purple hell out of her rear. She glared down at her sober partner and cleared her throat as Zoe sped through the introductions.

"Yes, yes." Violet Cooper waved Zoe's words out of the air with a slim, many-ringed hand that pinched the cigarette holder between thumb and forefinger. "Now, Zoefrieda," Violet began, "What is this important meeting about?"

Poppy carefully observed their flamboyant hostess. She sifted and stored information in her subconscious that would later surface when she began to draw her conclusions about who killed Nancy Marie Hightower.

Lupe spoke up first. "I will tell you, *mi dama*. I

22

must leave this place. I want to go to my family in the Valley. I am seventy-four years old. I am too old for working now and I have made my decision."

Violet shrunk. Her plumes sagged, the cigarette pointed at the floor. Her shoulders wilted. She lowered her head.

It was the best, the very damn *best* Lola Montez-Before-The-Blade that Poppy had ever seen. But, when Violet raised her head, Poppy was jolted by the raw pain she saw in those sad Dietrich eyes. A real woman lived in there. A woman who desperately wanted Lupe to stay, needed her to stay. But also a woman accustomed to the cruel turns of fate that robbed her of love and comfort, if not money.

Crawford shoulders came up, Hepburn spunk crackled in her eyes as Violet rose and gazed, faraway style, out the window. The star took one last hollow-cheeked suck on the cigarette, then stubbed it out for them with a fire-killing crunch. Poppy wrapped her fingers together to keep from applauding.

"All right, Lupe." Violet Cooper had it together now. Ida Lupino tough. Tendrils of white smoke still curled around her head. A perfect close-up shot, strong profile backlit by the window. "When will you leave? I must attend to finding someone to replace you."

Not waiting for an answer, Violet turned slowly and crossed stage right to where Marcie stood beside Poppy's chair. She extended a limp-wristed hand toward each of them. "Dahlings, as friends of Zoefrieda you are welcome at Red Rook. Please stay as long as you like — but you are wasting your time if you are here in your capacity as detectives."

23

The hands went away and clung to each other, one up — one down, in the nest of ostrich feathers. Then one flew up and waved the air.

Now who th' . . .?

Davis again, Dillworth. Sans ciggy-boo.

Right. Thanks.

"Because I'm certain that Nan ended her own life. I knew her." Step — wave. "Better . . . than . . . anyone."

Bet-tah . . . bet-tah . . . bet-tah! Poppy's mental comedienne echoed.

The actress paused. She sat, and then the real Violet Cooper appeared as an honest tear rolled down her cheek. "Oh, Lupe. I will miss you with all my heart. You are the only one left in the world who loves me. You are my *family*!"

Lupe went to Violet and hugged her, stroking her hair with a work-worn hand.

Poppy wished fervently for a fade-out and credits, but they would just have to live through this scene with no help from Cecil B. — painful though it was.

Zoe rescued them. "Violet — what about your Aunt Belle? Perhaps she could help us out. Since your Uncle Sherm passed away she's been kind of at loose ends, hasn't she? And I know Belle loves you."

Lupe smiled at Zoe. "Oh, yes. Wonderful."

Violet clasped her hands and stood. "Well, that is exactly the answer. I will go to Dallas and get her this very minute."

La dama grande and her faithful servant exited the sound stage, leaving a stunned audience of three behind.

Poppy lost it. She felt the giggle rise up in her

throat. It itched to get out. She felt her face redden under the scrutiny of the other two women.

"*Zoefrieda?*" she chortled, and ducked a well-aimed pillow.

– 3 –

Reruns and Previews

The rusty, camouflage-painted jeep bounced over the rocky road, sending Poppy's bottom clear of the back seat cushion for the third time. "Great Goddess, Zoe! Slow down, before we all go flying off this mountain!"

Gears clashed in response to Poppy's request as Zoe reduced speed.

"Oh, wow," Marcie gushed as they left the road and rolled to a stop just a few feet from a bluff. It looked out over the river about three hundred feet below and a quarter of a mile away.

"So this is where you found her, huh, Zoe?" Poppy asked, as she opened the case to her new video camera.

"Yeah. Right over there." Zoe gestured toward the lip of the drop-off.

"Now Zoe, what I want to do here is film and record you while you tell us exactly what you saw and did that day. Okay? So I can view it later in the VCR and compare your story with the report we're getting from the sheriff's office this afternoon." Poppy walked to the edge of the bluff with the camera, filming the view the dead woman had been facing. She turned slowly, panning, until she faced Marcie and Zoe who still stood by the jeep. "Okay, Zoe. You're up."

Zoe stuck her hands in her pockets, tensing up at the blinking red light on the camera that announced it was running. She walked self-consciously toward Poppy. "Well." She cleared her throat. "Well — uh, I was out real early that morning. The day after Halloween."

Poppy quickly calculated. Since this was the weekend after Thanksgiving, exactly four weeks had passed since Nan's death. Not much chance of finding any physical evidence.

Zoe continued. "I keep thinking — if it hadn't been for a pregnant heifer, I might've been able to prevent Nan's death. Maybe she called me to saddle Beau and I wasn't there. It wasn't like her to go off in the pickup on a morning like that one. She had a thing about the fall — about the first few frosty mornings when she could ride with all her new leather duds on. She did look pretty special — up on that big black horse, all dressed in black. Like a gunslinger, you know? Mean and sexy. I always kidded her about being Zorro. 'Specially when she wore her hat."

Zoe took a breath and removed her hands from the pockets of her sleeveless, fleece-lined vest. She tipped her gray Stetson back on her head as she ambled toward Poppy and the edge of the grassy area. "She liked to wear one of those Spanish-style, flat-topped, flat-brimmed hats. She thought it gave all the gals hot pants. She did look fine in it, though, like Barbara Stanwyck in *Big Valley* — only no skirts. Nan woulda died before she — uh —"

She stopped and looked out over the river for a moment, then down at the rock ledge just below her. "Well, all that's not important now. She did die." Zoe pointed down. "She was standing right about there, as I figure it, when it happened."

Poppy pointed the camera at the area Zoe had indicated, then stopped filming and asked, "Zoe — I'd like to try something, okay?"

"Sure, Pops."

"You say you think somebody murdered Nan. Well . . ." Poppy interrupted herself and cupped her hand by her mouth and shouted in the direction of the jeep. "Hey! Marcie. Come on over here!"

"You don't have to yell. I'm right here."

Both Poppy and Zoe jumped in surprise and turned to see the bright orange top of Marcie's knitted cap poking up above the edge of the rock ledge at their feet.

"You scared the bejusus out of me! How'd you get down there?" Poppy asked.

Marcie stepped out into view, still some feet from the outer lip of the flat outcropping. "I wandered into those trees up behind the jeep and found a trail and followed it down here. It looks like some sort of animals have used it." Marcie looked down at the rock she was standing on. "What did you want? I'm busy looking for clues — I mean evidence."

"I've got an idea. I need you to help me figure something out."

Poppy watched as Zoe grabbed Marcie's elbow and took a lot longer than was necessary to assist her around the lip of rock and over the edge.

Forget it, Wondercrone. There's nothing you can do about it. The child insists on wearing those grab-me sweaters over those twin torpedoes on her chest. Of course Zoe's gonna try for a free feel. What normal, red-blooded American lesbian cowgirl could resist that?

Poppy couldn't help emitting at least one quick disapproving snort. Zoe looked like she'd been caught up to the elbows in the cream churn, but Marcie seemed oblivious to any sounds save those coming from Zoe's lips.

"Ah — if I might have your attention here," Poppy said, an archness creeping into her voice. "Zoe, I want you to stand where you think Nan was that day. And I want you, Watson, to make believe you are the murderer. Try to act it out, see, for the camera."

"Yeah. Good idea, Poppy," Marcie answered. But her big brown eyes were still on Zoe.

"Here. Use this." Poppy drew a large water pistol made of clear chartreuse plastic from her jacket pocket and handed it to Marcie.

Zoe's face sobered immediately at the sight of the

mock weapon and she quickly took her position on the edge of the bluff.

Poppy hoisted the video camera to her shoulder, switched it on and squinted through the viewfinder. "Okay Zoe, take it slow now. Tell Marcie what to do. Show her how you think it happened."

Marcie handed Zoe the toy pistol and Zoe raised it to her temple.

"Here's how Sheriff Dumbass says it happened." She playacted a *bang*, tossed the gun down at her feet and lowered herself carefully to the ground. "This is how she was layin' when I found her, Pops."

Zoe moved around her, getting close-ups of Zoe and the immediate area. "Okay. You can get up now."

Zoe stood, brushing leaves from her faded 501s. "Dammit, Poppy, I *heard* the shot that killed her. I remember looking up here toward the ridge but I didn't see anything moving. I thought it was a deer hunter maybe, but the shot hadn't sounded right — not like a rifle at all."

Zoe's chin trembled and she looked at Poppy with moist questioning eyes. "I've racked my brain and I can't recall seeing or hearing anything out of the ordinary after that. Nothing . . . and while I was loading that damned stubborn teenage cow in the trailer, Nan's murderer got clean away."

"It's too late for ifs and buts," Poppy interrupted brusquely. "What we *can* do now, though, is see if we can bring Nan's killer to justice."

Zoe's chin stopped its quiver as she straightened her back and looked at Poppy with renewed determination. "You're absolutely right, Pops. Okay,

Marcie babe, you take this gun now, and I'll show you what to do with it."

Babe? Hoo-boy. Got the jingle back in our spurs now, don't we, Buckaroo?

Marcie allowed Zoe to position her body to the left of her and check the bearings all around them, then Poppy zoomed up close with the picture as Marcie raised the pistol and *banged* at Zoe's temple.

"That's it Poppy. Plain and simple," Zoe said toward the camera. "Someone just shot her. I can't figure how they coulda sneaked up on her but maybe they did. If it was someone she knew, maybe they were up here talking and the killer had the gun hidden and surprised her or something. That's another thing that bothers me, though. Why would she come off way up here to meet someone? She always had an affair going with some woman or other — but I think she put the lid on all that after Morgana came on the scene. And she just wasn't dressed for that kind of meeting. Y'know what I mean?"

Marcie looked at Zoe with sudden interest. "How long after you heard the shot did you actually discover the body?" Marcie asked.

"Well, when I got back to the cabin just before noon to clean up for lunch, Violet was camped out on my front stoop. Seems like Nan's lawyer from Dallas had called, wanting to know how come Nan hadn't showed up for an eleven o'clock appointment." Zoe removed her hat and ran a hand briskly through her hair. For Marcie's benefit, Poppy was sure. Then she continued. "Violet was hopping mad, too, because Nan hadn't told her about seeing the lawyer and she wanted to know if I'd seen Nan and if *I* knew anything about the reason for Nan's appointment."

Poppy continued to record voice and picture, as Zoe went on with her story. "Well, I told you — I couldn't get back in the jeep fast enough, but I managed to get Violet off to the big house by suggesting that someone should be by the phone if Nan called. My heart was thumping so hard I thought I was gonna be sick before I got up here to the bluff. I kept hearing that shot over and over again in my mind."

Zoe dropped to a cowhand squat — one bony knee up, the other down — and whipped the toe of her boot with a long blade of seeded grass. She looked up at Marcie, then at Poppy, apparently struggling to maintain composure. "I'm not psychic by a long shot, but I knew — I just *knew* something bad had happened to Nan. When I got up here where I thought I heard the shot, I parked right behind her pickup and started looking around. Of course it didn't take me but a few seconds to spot her. I ran over and bent down to feel for her pulse but I didn't even touch her. It was easy enough to see she was dead."

Zoe stood suddenly and turned away. Her shoulders jerked slightly as she brought her emotions under control. Marcie went to Zoe's side and slipped a comforting arm around her waist. They stood there still for a moment. Poppy panned the horizon in a complete circle, waiting for her friend to go on with her painful story.

"I went to Nan's pickup and got the blanket she always kept behind the seat for emergencies. I put it over her and went back to the house to call the sheriff's office. I coulda used the phone in Nan's pickup — but I knew I had to tell Violet and Lupe in person. And Nan was dead . . . no amount of hurry from the sheriff's office was going to help *her*." Zoe walked toward the jeep and leaned against it. Marcie's hand remained in Zoe's. Poppy followed them with her camera.

"Lupe made Violet take a tranquilizer. She'd thrown a million-dollar hissy when I told her about Nan, but by the time Swindell and his clowns got there, she'd calmed down and taken to her bed."

Zoe helped Marcie up into the passenger seat of the jeep and stood on the ground beside her, patting Marcie's plump knee as she finished her tale. "I led that bunch of idiots up here and they proceeded to trample down any kind of evidence that might've been here. They just fishtailed that county Ford and the firehouse ambulance up beside Nan's pickup and pounded the ground flat in about two minutes. That no-neck deputy that was filling in for Bubba even took a *leak* off the cliff there before they ever got Nan's body on the stretcher!"

Zoe's face reddened as her anger grew. "The sonuvabitch even said, ' I've heard these *homaseckshal* women is always bumping themselves off. Looks like money don't make no difference.' " She jutted her jaw out at Poppy. "They had their minds made up before they left the ranch."

Poppy swung the camera off her aching shoulder and clambered past Marcie into the back seat. "Well, let's not waste a good mad on remembering. Let's get into town and talk to the good ole boys."

"You got it," Zoe answered, and headed the jeep

back down the rocky trail. A mile or so later Zoe turned onto another road. It was still on the ranch, though, as far as Poppy could tell.

"This'll take us to town a little quicker than going back to the house," Zoe explained.

The road wound through the red-orange land like a wrinkled ribbon. Through dry washes, over brushy hills and around ponds where flocks of winter birds rose into the azure sky, complaining at the jeep's intrusion.

Zoe pointed across Marcie's nose and said, "That's the Drake place over there. The Drakes and the Hightowers have owned this land in unbroken succession for over a hundred years. All that's gonna change now, though, with Nan gone."

"How's that?" Poppy asked.

"Well, there's no more Hightowers except for J.C. Junior, and if my hunch is right about him, he's lost any chance he might've ever had to inherit anything. Nan's father disinherited him when he ducked the draft. Completely. There's even a little square hole in the family Bible where his name was."

"Pretty drastic, wouldn't you say?" asked Marcie.

"Nan never thought so. See — J.C. Senior was a big World War II hero. You'll see when we get to town. There's a statue down at the court house with his name on it." Zoe stopped talking as she carefully guided the jeep across a small creek studded with large round rocks. "He didn't last five years after Junior left. Nan said he died of a broken heart. Could be. He died from a heart *attack* anyhow."

"What about Nan's mother? What happened to her?" Marcie asked.

"Well — she never was much use, according to

Nan. And I can agree with that. She was pretty much in an alcoholic haze any time I ever saw her. She roared off in her big old Lincoln Continental one day and tried to pass a hay truck just before she got to the main highway to town. Met a county gravel truck head on. Going about eighty, they figured. Whole mess caught fire — hay and all."

They topped a small hill and the landscape began to change colors. Bright green fields of winter wheat rolled away toward the horizon. The remaining stretch of ranch road was now visible up to the corner where it joined the pavement. A large, boxy Mercedes truck lumbered toward them on the other side of the fence.

"What in the world is that guy doing out here? Reckon he's lost?" Poppy asked, in surprise.

"Nope. He's heading for Bitsy's studio. Bitsy Drake. Collin's daughter. She makes some kinda stuff for museums." The truck came even with the jeep and quickly disappeared behind them on its opposite course.

Zoe continued. "And that's the reason the Drake land won't continue to be owned by the Drakes. Bitsy's his only child and she's a real Looney Tune. Lives by herself in that lonesome A-frame across from the old home place down by the river. Nan said she was a nutty kind of a kid. Used to go with Junior. Real bright in school — got scholarships to art college, all that, but came back here after graduation and got her daddy to build her that studio. I think they live off the money she makes, but he hovers around and protects her like some old lone wolf. Every once in a while she used to come to town for supplies and stuff, but she quit even that a few years

35

back. I guess Collin gets her what she needs. She's known as Ditsy Bitsy around here."

"Oh, look, Poppy," Marcie exclaimed, pointing at a group of picturesque ranch buildings clustered in a grove of nearly bare trees. "Isn't that wonderful? Just like a movie set!"

"That's Collin Drake's house," Zoe said.

"Stop, Zoe. I want to get it on tape." Marcie looked pleadingly at Poppy.

"Sure, Sugarpie." Poppy couldn't help grinning at her partner's youthful exuberance. She handed the video camera to Marcie as Zoe slowed the jeep to a stop. "Here — make sure you've got it on."

Poppy stepped out and stretched while Marcie pointed the camera in the direction of the old weather-beaten ranch house and barns. The fences were tight though, Poppy observed, as her eyes swept down the taut strands of barbed wire. The place was weathered to a uniform gray — no paint at all remained, but it didn't seem to be ramshackle or in disrepair otherwise.

A crow flapped skyward from its perch on a post and cawed its disapproval of the moviemakers into the crisp, clear morning air. A tall male figure emerged from an outbuilding, strode across an open yard, turned in their direction once, then disappeared into the house.

"Ditsy Bitsy's father, I presume?" Poppy asked.

"Yeah. That's him, poor guy," Zoe replied and stood open mouthed, observing Marcie with obvious pleasure as Marcie finished her taping and handed the camera back to Poppy.

"Well, y'all ready to go?" Zoe asked and grinned

guiltily when she realized Poppy had caught her ogling Marcie's well-filled sweater.

As Zoe ground the key into the moving ignition, Poppy said archly, "I believe the engine's still running, Zoe*frieda*." Then she settled into the back seat and added, "Let's go see Sheriff Dumbass." She noted happily that Zoe's ears had begun to glow deep red.

– 4 –
The Good, the Bad,
and the Difference

A ceiling fan turned slowly, evenly distributing odious cigarette smoke to all sections of the Courthouse Cafe — *Cindy Lou and Bobby Lynn Baker, Proprietors.* Poppy, Marcie and Zoe sat at a round booth in the corner with a thin young man in a tan uniform. Poppy squared up the sheaf of papers beside her plate of home fries and gravy. "Deputy Swin—" she began.

"Oh. Please. Just call me Bubba. There's too many Swindells in the sheriff's office. It's folks' way of keeping us separate. Besides, I'd rather be called Bubba than Delbert Augustine." He smiled winningly at the three women.

"Uh — okay . . . Bubba." Poppy somehow made her lips say it without smiling. "And you say this is a complete copy of your file on the Hightower case?"

"Yes ma'am, it is. Whups, I did it again. Red'll kill me if I don't start remembering to ask females what they'd rather be called. I mean, does *ma'am* bother y'all?" He looked at Marcie and Poppy. Poppy supposed he'd already covered this point of etiquette with Zoe.

"That's just fine . . . Bubba." Poppy grinned at the earnest young man.

"Well, Red — Beverly, my wife — she's a feminist and she says its politically incorrect to call females by titles like ma'am and endearments like honey and darlin', but it still just seems to me like *ma'am* is being respectful."

Bubba ran out of words and toyed with a small red-nosed reindeer from the holiday centerpiece that took up most of the middle of their table. Suddenly remembering more etiquette, he stood abruptly and held his huge nickel-plated pistol and holster out at right angles, dug in his pocket for a second and produced a white business card.

"Here's my card." He thrust it at Poppy, but he lost his hold on the leather-encased pistol, beeper, handcuffs and other accoutrements of sheriffing

39

attached to his belt. The ensuing whoosh and clatter knocked the card into Poppy's plate.

He darted a hand toward it but Poppy waved him back as if he were a poorly trained pup. "That's okay, Bubba. I got it." She smiled at him, licked gravy from the card and put it in her shirt pocket.

"Honest, Sugarpie. Don't worry about it." She looked up at Deputy Sheriff Swindell, who still stood beside the table like a jackrabbit frozen in a spotlight. "Let's finish up our lunch. I've got a few questions I'd like to ask but I'm too hungry to concentrate."

Bubba sat and gratefully resumed his attack on a double chili cheeseburger and chocolate malt. Poppy cast a glance sideways at Marcie and Zoe. Their apparent mutual enjoyment of both the food and each other's company reminded Poppy of the eating scene from *Tom Jones.*

Shoulda sat between 'em, Dillworth. There's kneesies going on under this table or my radar's out of whack!

"Delbert!" A piercing voice halted the chewing motion of Bubba's jaws and Poppy watched, amazed, as he swallowed a barely chewed mouthful in one frog-like gulp. The voice continued as its owner rapidly approached. "I have to go to Dallas and help out at the Women's Shelter Christmas party. I been trying to get in touch with you all morning. Surely some of that stuff you got hanging off you is turned *on,* isn't it?" The tall, heavy-set young woman with red-orange hair turned her attention from the errant Bubba to Poppy, Marcie and Zoe. She brightened, visibly, at the prospect of what Poppy guessed she

40

thought to be other like-minded victims of the patriarchy, ripe for evangelizing.

"Howdy." She stuck out a pink hand, now freed of its politically correct, all-cotton weave, made-in-a-third-world-country mitten. "I'm Beverly Baxter-Swindell." She made scoot-waves at Bubba with her mitten, and sat on the edge of the curved bench seat.

Poppy stifled her amusement after she caught a glimpse of Bubba's miserable face. Something deep within her stirred from an almost dormant state and awakened into a growling, full-grown mama grizzly. It rose up and hovered protectively over Bubba's sloping shoulders. Then it prompted Poppy off the seat a little, pushed her hand forward to grasp Baxter-Hyphen-Swindell's pink hand in a bone-crunching grip.

"Howdy back atcha," Poppy barked, still squeezing. "I'm Papillon Audubon Dillworth. This is my partner Miz Marcie Louise Judy and I reckon you already know our good friend Miz Zoefrieda Zentmeyer." The mama grizzly grinned around the table, sat and stuffed an appropriately bear-sized forkful of gravy-covered home fries into her mouth. She relished the look of surprised gratitude in the young deputy's eyes and the open-mouthed amazement on Zoe's face. In fifteen years, Zoe had never been able to dig Poppy's full name out of her, and now she'd dropped it like a cup of frosty punch right into Red Swindell's lap.

Bubba's brief rescue was short-lived, however, as Red turned her attention to the greasy dripping

41

burger he still clutched with both hands. "You know that stuff'll kill you, Delbert." She turned to inform the women. *"Cholesterol."* She uttered the dreaded word in hushed disapproval and it hung in the air over the table like a teacher with an upraised ruler.

Zoe was selected as next target. "How is Morgana's organic beef project coming along?"

Zoe held the remainder of a yeast roll in her hand and eyed Poppy's leftover gravy. Poppy shoved the plate in her direction with an indulgent smile. Zoe answered tersely while she chased the last bit of cream gravy around the bright blue plate with another roll. "I don't believe it ever got past the 'what if' stage. Nan wasn't too much in favor of it, anyhow."

Poppy's sense of timing said *now* and she poked Marcie in the soft roll of flesh that covered her ribs, then she raised an eyebrow and spoke to Bubba. "Why don't you and me go over to the Sheriff's office, Bubba, while my partner here, Detective Judy, interviews your wife." She nodded in Red's direction. "That is, if you have the time, Ms. Swindell. We'd like to get a few facts straight about Morgana's interest in Red Rook Ranch. My partner and I have been engaged to investigate the possibility of murder in the Hightower case."

Red's unplucked eyebrows rose in an unbridled display of interest and she glowed rays of helpfulness as Marcie placed the tiny black tape recorder on the table and dug a notepad from her pocket.

Poppy and the Deputy excused themselves and quickly made their way through the noon crowd to the cash register. Poppy beamed at Cindy Lou, the waitressing half of the Baker team, and said, "That's the best damn gravy I've had since I last tasted my mama's." She paid for her and Marcie's lunch and got a receipt for taxes. "Be sure and tell Bobby Lynn what I said about the gravy," she repeated, and waved back at the extended change tray. "Just keep it, honey, that's yours." She saw Bubba's head jerk just a little as she tossed the incorrect endearment in with her tip.

"Y'all come back *real* soon." Cindy Lou smiled and winked broadly at Poppy as she folded the five and tucked it neatly into her cleavage.

They walked slowly down the sidewalk while Poppy managed to regear her knee joints from sitting to walking. She glanced at the puzzled expression of the earnest young man walking with her. "Don't break your head trying to figure it out, son. It's not so much *what* you say, but *where* your heart *is* when you say it."

They walked companionably beneath the corrugated tin awnings that jutted out from various storefronts along one side of the square. The circa-1880 red stone courthouse rose over them like a Disney set, replete with gargoyles and cupolas and clock-tower. Blackened iron hitching posts still served as delimiters for the yellowed winter-grass lawns surrounding the aged building. Sure enough, as Zoe had promised, a green-streaked statue of a soldier stood beside the main steps. Poppy stopped in front of it to read the pink granite slab at its foot. The first of six names after the WWI legend read *Phineas Barry Hightower, Sgt., U.S. Army, Distinguished Service Cross, 1918, France,* and the first of a long list after WWII read *Lt. Joseph Calvin Hightower, U.S.M.C. — Tarawa, W.C. Pacific, 1943 — Purple*

Heart. Then there was a long list for Vietnam. Even two for Korea, Poppy noted, but no more Hightowers.

She climbed the wide bank of worn marble steps to where Bubba braved domestic wrath and held the door open for her. They traversed a cavernous drafty hall festooned with lengths of tinsel rope that had seen too many seasons of service, past a twinkling tree on a kiosk with a banner asking passersby to bring toys for the Firehouse Children's Party.

Brave Bubba again held a door open, and this time it led Poppy into the nostalgic past. A drooping, dusty, gold-fringed banner hung from the ceiling behind an unbelievably cluttered desk. The ubiquitous pointed star against the blue background of the flag announced Rojo County Sheriff's Department. Two men in tan uniforms bent over a large map draped across a side table, but they rose in tandem as they noticed Poppy behind Bubba. A graying woman, same tan uniform, paused in her typing to peer at Poppy over her glasses, then resumed her speedy clatter.

Goddamn — it even smells the same!. Poppy's gut rolled at the memories of a lifetime of sitting in that clerk's chair, looking at the world happen outside her sphere, of wanting — *needing* — to find some validation — some personhood in the world of, for, and by men.

Remember, Irma, how I used to cry and curse and pound the walls in frustration? Barely hanging on till retirement? And how you held me when all I could do was cry? God, I need you now so much to help me celebrate this freedom. It's not fair! Why did you die and leave me alone?

She fought down an impulse to turn and leave.

44

She made herself listen to Bubba's halting introductions.

"Hi there, little lady, pleased to meetcha," said the white-haired, red-nosed replica of Bubba. He stuck out a spotty blue-veined hand. "Just call me Pappy, Poppy," he said, then chuckled, happy with his own wittiness.

"And hi *there*, old fella, likewise." Poppy squeezed hard in silent anger at being called "little lady" and winced at the unexpected calloused hardness of the old man's hand.

The middle-aged version of Bubba then took *his* turn at the end of Poppy's arm. "Highdee, Miz Dillworth. Everybody just calls me Bert — or Sheriff. We got a real unusual situation here, with three generations of Swindells still in service." He clapped Bubba on the shoulder. "M'boy here got hisself married to a big old red-haired gal some time back. Thought we might have number four in here by now, but he ain't give me any red-on-the-head grandbabies yet." He looked accusingly at his son.

Poppy felt the hole in her gut close up tight as the mama grizzly shifted and opened her eyes. It was easier to deal with these maternal instincts since the bear's appearance. *Hunh-unh Griz, not now. We got work to do.* She made herself look at Sheriff Bert instead of the crestfallen and embarrassed Bubba. She cleared her throat, indicating the ball was in Bert's court.

"Well!" he began, as Pappy went back to the wrinkled map. "M'boy here tells me you're bound and determined to prove us wrong about the Hightower suicide."

45

Bubba squared his shoulders a little and bowed his neck like a dog about to engage in an often played game of bite and tug. "Dad, you know I disagree with you and Pap on this one. There's just too many things that don't add up. I've told Miz Dillworth I'd help her if I could."

"Well, you'll have to do it on your own time. You know we got our hands full with the body parts them boys found over at the gravel pit." He turned to Poppy. "Who you workin' for? Cowboy Zentmeyer?"

Poppy didn't miss the clear distaste in Sheriff Bert's voice. "Yes," she answered in a tone so even and strong it brought Pappy's head up sharply from his map study. "Miz Zoefrieda Zentmeyer has retained me and my partner, Miz Judy, to find Nan Hightower's murderer. And we aim to do just that. With or without the assistance of this . . . department." She noticed the typing had stopped.

The sheriff considered her briefly — looking her up and down with a firm press-suck of his thin lips. Apparently deciding she was not worth the breath it would take to comment, he turned to Bubba and said, "That wife of yours was seen in Dallas last week talking to that California queer again at the Women's Shelter. You need to rein her in, boy." He walked purposefully across to the table and joined Pappy at the map. "Or you ain't *ever* goin' to get any babies." He sat and resumed finger-tracing the map, clearly dismissing Poppy and his apparently spineless offspring.

Bubba, now poinsettia-red, turned on his heel and stalked out the door. Poppy followed him down the hall and out into the sunny December afternoon.

Okay, Griz. Now. She took Bubba's elbow firmly

46

in her hand and looped her arm around it, patting, talking and walking at the same time. "Don't fret, son. Let's just keep our minds and our energies concentrated on solving this puzzle, okay?"

Bubba's face relaxed a little as he grinned thinly at her. "Okay. Uh . . . I got to go to work now though. The cafe's right down there." He pointed down the street where Poppy noticed Zoe and Marcie just coming out.

"Hey —" She poked his shoulder. "I'm not so old and feeble-minded I can't remember the way back!"

"Oh. I'm sorry, ma'am. I didn't mean anything — I get so — he just makes me . . ."

She cut him off. "I know, son. Like I said, don't worry about it. Go on, now." She shooed him away. "Bye. And thanks for the report. I know you took a chance giving it to me." She meaningfully tapped her boxy black leather purse.

Bubba disappeared behind the tinted glass window of a jet-black Chevrolet Suburban parked head-in at the curb. A gold circled star on its door proclaimed it as an official vehicle of the Rojo County Sheriff's Department.

As Poppy strode toward the cafe and her two friends, she noticed the big Mercedes truck from that morning gassing up at the Fina station just down from the square. A lanky man with a ponytail snaking out from under his red *gimme* hat slowly washed the windows of the pug-faced cab.

Folks around here don't get in much of a hurry, she thought, as her eyes picked out the big green Sinclair Oil dinosaur on the sign behind the truck. Sinclair's been dead almost as long as its logo.

She joined Zoe and Marcie where they stood

47

window-shopping. "C'mon, pardners." She nudged Marcie and motioned Zoe toward the end of the street where the jeep was parked. "Let's get back out to the ranch and go over this report Bubba gave us."

Poppy followed Zoe and Marcie down the sidewalk past Smith's Rexall drugstore and turned toward the rows of vehicles crowded into the narrow parking lot by the feed store. Zoe squeezed into the jeep and wrestled the steering wheel, making little up and back cuts as she cursed the Christmas shoppers that had almost blocked the jeep into its space beside the red brick wall. Finally free, she inched out onto the makeshift driveway so Poppy and Marcie could climb aboard.

Poppy was quiet on the drive out of town, processing impressions, pictures and private thoughts stirred up by the unsettling visit to the sheriff's office. She was aware, on various levels, of the passing countryside, of Marcie and Zoe sitting a little too close together and of her mind clinking away — sorting ideas and questions, points to be covered in the investigation.

"Sonuvabitch!" Zoe exploded into action on the seat in front of her. "The goddamn brakes are gone!" She stomped her boot futilely on the pedal and jerked on the hand brake but the jeep didn't slow down.

"Hold on — we're in deep shit," she warned as the jeep gathered speed down the steep hill. "There's nowhere to go but the creek down there on the curve!"

Poppy tightened her seat belt and clutched her purse to her chest.

"Hang on! This is our only chance!" Zoe steered onto the shoulder of the road and aimed at the bar-ditch between the road and the adjoining field. Poppy held her breath in horror as the hurtling jeep followed the ditch briefly, then Knieveled over a cattle guard at an adjoining hay-truck lane and sailed into the pasture, bumping through thick brush, thankfully slowing as Zoe efficiently maneuvered the vehicle onto more level land.

"Damn!" Zoe exclaimed as they rolled to a stop then started moving slowly in the opposite direction. She quickly shifted into reverse and popped out the clutch, killing the engine with a quick turn of the key. Finally — they were still.

Poppy breathed again and unsnapped her seat belt and Zoe hugged Marcie. Zoe turned a wide-eyed face toward Poppy and said quietly, "Pops — I got a funny feeling this was *no* accident."

Poppy nodded her agreement and tapped Marcie's rigid shoulder. "Sugarpie — I think Zoe's right on the mark. You still got that fingerprint kit in your saddlebag?"

– 5 –
Where There's A Will . . .

Poppy's knees ached from yesterday's harrowing ride in the jeep. They'd had to walk back to the ranch gates where Zoe had called for Rick, her top hand, to bring the big John Deere tractor down so they could get the jeep back to the vehicle barn.

After it was raised on the lift, Zoe had stood under the jeep and pointed out to Poppy where the brake lines had been partially cut, perhaps with a hacksaw, and showed her how easily the cable on the hand brake had slipped from its mooring after a locknut had been loosened. Although the undercarriage of the old jeep was too oily and dirty to yield any fingerprints, the recent tool marks were obvious where the bright metal shone through the grime.

After taking photos, they had called Bubba Swindell who came to look at the jeep and take their report. It looked to him, Bubba had said, like they were lucky to be alive. Poppy agreed. Someone did not want them asking questions about Nan Hightower's death. This put an entirely new face on the whole affair.

Poppy, Marcie and Zoe were drinking coffee and discussing strategy at Zoe's kitchen table when the intercom from the house crackled, then buzzed loudly. Zoe rubbed her hands together nervously, pressed a red button and spoke. "Yes — I'm here — go ahead."

Lupe's usually controlled voice held a note of excitement as she instructed Zoe: "The ladies arrived early and are all settled in now. Miss Violet wishes me to tell you that as soon as Mr. Barnes arrives we will have the reading of the will!"

"All right, Lupe. Thanks — we'll be right up."

Poppy rose from the table, tucked the tail of her red plaid flannel shirt into her black denim pants, and slipped on the long black sweater vest that Irma had given her their last Christmas together. As she examined her appearance in a hall mirror she fingered the bear-claw that hung around her neck on

51

a heavy silver chain and ran a hand through her curly white hair. *Okay, ole blue eyes — let's get this show on the road.*

"C'mon Marcie!" she shouted at the door to the bathroom. "Anything over three wipes is playing!"

Marcie emerged, red-faced, into the hallway and flounced huffily toward the door. Zoe grabbed her hat and dashed to open it for her, sending Poppy a meaningful glare as she did so.

Uh-oh. This is beginning to look serious. Guess I need to have a private talk with my little buddy Marcie — see if that big ole bad ole butch has been doing anything besides looking.

* * * * *

The sun shone mightily, burning white in the clear blue sky. Just a little north breeze was left from the cold front. A big dome of high pressure had moved into place and appeared likely to remain for a couple of days. Poppy was glad, as she had some field work to do and didn't look forward to out-of-doors surveillance even in the best of weather.

As they neared the house Zoe announced, "Well — goddamn. There's Barnes getting out of that Continental and lookee who's coming up behind him!" She pointed at a brilliant lavender VW bug just coming to a sliding stop in the circular drive. They all watched as a stunning blonde dressed in a revealing, electric purple leotard pulled a multicolored cape around her shoulders and stopped for a moment in conversation with a very tall man in flamboyant western attire.

"The bew-chus Morgana?" Poppy prompted.

"Yep — the one and greedy only," Zoe answered, as she made hurry motions toward the back door. "*Rapido muchachas* — let's get in there. I wanna see the fireworks when Violet finds out Morgana is here!"

Zoe led them into a long airy room with beamed ceilings. Several low, comfortable sofas and armchairs were grouped in front of a mammoth stone fireplace that took up the whole end of the room. A heavy, primitively carved mantlepiece jutted out over a glowing fire. It held bright pots with intricate designs and served as the base for a huge, framed map. A very old map from the look of the spidery Spanish lettering on it.

The three women had just settled onto one of the outer sofas when the soft pealing of bells signaled the arrival of guests. Poppy checked the recorder in her pocket and positioned her finger on the *record* button, ready for action.

Which wasn't long in coming.

The Lawyer and The Blonde had no more than entered the room behind Lupe when Violet Cooper, Star-In-Mourning, burst onto the scene, dressed in dramatic black from head to boot. She took one look at Morgana and wilted onto a sofa.

Poppy punched the button as the show began and fastened her eyes on a small energetic woman who hovered over the swooning Violet. A sixtyish woman with a single long braid of thick white hair. A woman with flashing brown eyes and the profile of an aging diva. A woman who made Poppy's heart beat a bit faster than was attributable to the histrionics of the moment. Poppy knew she should concentrate on the dynamics of the eclectic group of people, but somehow

53

her attention remained riveted on the lithe little woman who now took Violet in charge and quieted her with a firm, matter-of-fact, no-nonsense manner.

"Snap to, Vi," the woman said as she waved something under the Bereaved Widow's nose. "Straighten up here, this won't do." She turned to the others as Violet sat sniffing loudly behind her. "I'm Belle Stoner. Violet is my niece. If everyone will take a seat perhaps we can get on with the business of the will." She took Morgana by the elbow and seated her downstage left, out of Violet's line of sight but still very much inside the circle of participants.

The man in the business version of a cowboy suit cleared his throat, extracted a document from his briefcase, and took center stage. "How do you do. I'm Cletus Barnes. Attorney for the deceased, Nancy Marie Hightower. The following is her last will and testament, signed in my presence on the thirteenth day of October of this year."

Violet gasped.

Morgana smiled smugly.

Zoe said, "But that's less than two months ago. Just two days before she died!"

Barnes removed his stylish gold-rimmed aviator glasses and looked at Zoe as he cleaned them meticulously with a large handkerchief. "That's correct, Ms. Zentmeyer. Nancy had come to me with some significant changes the week before and she signed them, as you say, just two days before she passed away."

Poppy noted the varying reactions of the interested parties. She watched with quickening interest as Belle Stoner took a seat beside Violet and patted her niece's hand reassuringly. Then suddenly

54

Belle jumped to her feet as an enormous gray and white cat walked purposefully across the room and began sniffing inspection of Cletus Barnes' hand-tooled leather briefcase.

Belle picked up her pet, admonishing, "Cleopatra — naughty girl!" The tension momentarily lessened in the room as she returned to her seat, her arms full of the furry animal. "I'm sorry — please go on."

No sooner had the lawyer begun intoning the legalese of the various bequests, than the cat slipped from Belle's grasp and padded across the thick carpet, seeming not so much to walk as to glide toward Poppy. She stopped, sat, and looked inquiringly up at Poppy from yellow-green, almond-shaped eyes outlined in black. The short snowy hair of her muzzle followed the outline of her mouth, indenting in a natural smile. A thin band of white contrasted sharply with the black under each eye, giving her a slight resemblance to Liz in her namesake movie. Sparkling white tufts of hair sprouted from each ear, almost begging to be smoothed and fussed between thumb and forefinger. Cleopatra was indeed an attractive cat. Even a dog-woman like Poppy had to concede that.

Poppy shifted in her seat, a little uncomfortable under such intense feline scrutiny. The cat must have read the move as a signal of invitation, for she leaped nimbly into Poppy's lap and stretched herself along Poppy's thighs. Her big, white back paws stretched out toward the room and her fluffy, white front paws rested firmly against Poppy's pubic bone. She looked again at Poppy, rolled her head until it rested against Poppy's abdomen, and then closed her eyes and waited, Poppy supposed, to be petted.

Well goddamn — helluva note!

Since it was almost impossible to hold the silky animal and not stroke it, and because Belle Stoner was looking at her with a surprised, pleased expression, Poppy moved her hand cautiously over Cleopatra's gray fur. Her other hand was soon seduced into action.

Poppy's attention was suddenly gripped by the tension in the room as Barnes finished with the lesser items in the will and cleared his throat importantly.

"And to my much loved Violet, I leave the main ranch compound, including the immediately surrounding grounds — all that property inside the white fences. She is to have one half of all my holdings."

Barnes paused and tapped a fold of the long computer print-out. "There's an itemized listing here, Ms. Cooper, but in consideration of brevity I won't read it."

Violet nodded. Her expression, it seemed to Poppy, indicated a sort of faint held in check by shock and curiosity.

The cat stretched in Poppy's lap, stood, and turned her tail toward Poppy, curling it into a fluffy question mark that trailed across Poppy's upper lip, down the side of her face and under her chin, three times in quick succession, like a painter delineating a troublesome line. Then she hunkered down again and began to knead the pads of her front paws into the soft flesh of Poppy's inner knee. Tiny pinpricks secured Poppy's immediate attention.

Now what th'?

She grasped Cleo's paws gently but firmly and separated them from her leg, then distracted the cat by scratching her behind the ears. A loud, slurpy, rattling sound rose from the cat's chest — louder and louder until Barnes stopped talking and everyone in the room stared at Poppy. She felt her ears heat up, then her face, as Cleo continued to indulge herself in a fit of exhibitionistic purring.

Belle laughed, her eyes sparkling with something, Poppy thought, close to mischief. "Excuse me." She looked around the room. "Cleo, you bad girl!" she admonished her pet as she took her from Poppy's knees and disappeared down the hall for a moment. She returned alone to her place beside Violet.

Poppy's lap was suddenly cold and empty, and she jammed her hands in her sweater pockets, trying not to look at Zoe, who was almost doubled over with silent glee.

Barnes continued with the reading. The oil holdings were dispersed well by well — each one called out by name and lease number. As there were over two hundred, this effort took some time. But Poppy had been counting and knew only a hundred and four had been addressed when Barnes took a deep breath, looked around the room, and then began to read the bequest to Lupe of a generous income for life plus paid-up medical insurance.

Poppy noted that Violet the Accountant had taken over. She was making notes and tic marks in a ledger spread across her knees. She too had been counting and seemed extremely agitated as Barnes went on.

"And to my friend Zoe Zentmeyer, I give the two hundred acres by the river known as the Bottoms, the six wells on that property and one pair each of the breeding stock, both horses and cattle. She is to have first choice of animals."

Zoe's face paled at the unexpected largesse of her bequest and she grinned shakily at Poppy. Barnes stopped to reclean his glasses and to sip from the water glass on the low table by his chair, then continued.

"And lastly, I leave to Stephanie Alice Michaels, known as Morgana, the remaining lands of Red Rook Ranch, especially that part known as the old home place and the guest house near there. All the oil wells not previously mentioned and all of my stocks, bonds and investments to be held in a trust for the care of a child born of Morgana — sired by my brother Joseph Calvin Hightower, Junior. This child to be raised as my own, with all the benefits and rights accorded an heir. If Morgana and/or the child precede me in death the aforementioned properties are to be dispersed according to the wording of my original will." Barnes paused, and nodded in Violet's direction. "Meaning they would revert to you Ms. Cooper."

Violet leaped to her feet, shouting at Morgana. "My God! What did you talk my poor Nan into? How can you dare to call yourself a witch? You are an *evil* woman!" Her face paled and she stumbled back into her seat, with Belle and Lupe in attendance.

Appearing a bit rattled, Barnes continued to speak. "If Morgana chooses to live apart from me or chooses a mate other than myself, she will forfeit all benefit of the aforementioned trust and the child will be called upon to choose where it will live. If it chooses to go with Morgana, it too will forfeit all rights to Red Rook Ranch. My brother, Joseph Calvin Hightower, Junior, is to receive one hundred thousand dollars for his services as sperm donor expressly for the purposes of a successful artificial insemination. No other rights of kinship or rights to the child are intended or should be assumed."

Morgana lifted her chin righteously under the stress of scrutiny by every eye in the room. "Nan wanted a baby and I intend to produce one for her. The child was part of her dream of dynasty — a part of the Hightower blood that will live on. I have information that leads me to believe Joseph will be found and I will fulfill Nan's desire for a child."

She turned to Zoe. "I intend to move into the guest house immediately. You may reach me there from now on. I will also want to use Beauregard as my personal animal. I'll call when I need him saddled."

Zoe's face reddened and her jaws clenched and unclenched. "Like hell you will! The General is registered breeding stock and you're not gettin' your greedy hands on him!" She crossed her arms over her middle and glared at Morgana.

"We'll see," Morgana answered drily.

"Please, ladies, let's not indulge in spats," Barnes refereed over his glasses.

"Oh, balls!" Zoe exploded, leaping to her feet, ignoring Barnes. "I don't know what you did to Nan, but ever since you showed up, nothin's been the same. Nobody wants you here. Why don't you just pack up your crystals and catch the next broom back to California?"

Zoe stalked from the room. Everyone sat in shocked silence. Poppy figured Barnes had just about rubbed a hole in one lens of his glasses.

Lupe stood, hovering protectively over Violet, and spoke quietly. "I have decided not to leave. I will stay

59

here as long as *mi dama* needs me." She turned to Morgana. "Zoe is right. You are not wanted here."

Right on cue, Violet rose from her seat. But the silver screen played no part in the performance she gave. The true grit of Violet Cooper, wronged woman, faithful lover of Nan Hightower, shone through like search lights on a Hollywood opening night. She addressed Morgana.

"It has always been my dream to build a retirement house on the old home place by the river, for Nan and me. Nan *knew* how I felt about that place. She must have loved you very much to disappoint me so deeply. I always thought she would return to me in the end. And she always *did* until *you* came into her life."

Real tears crept down Violet's face. Her shoulders dropped briefly, then came up as determination seemed to flash through her. "So be it! I know Nan wanted children, though never enough to have them herself. *I* would have given her a child . . . but I am past the age. Go — do what you must. But stay out of my sight. I don't ever want to look at you again!"

– 6 –
. . . There's A Way

Poppy glanced up at the rear-view mirror in the cab of the little R.V. The mirror was useless for its intended purpose — the extended side mirrors filled that need very well — but it did afford a view of the woman who sat talking excitedly in the bucket seat beside hers.

What a profile. Those eyes. Poppy sighed inwardly. Belle Stoner was vivacious, earthy, witty, intelligent, beautiful . . . and straight.

The miles peeled away behind them. Poppy even welcomed the slowdown caused by the omnipresent construction north of the city. Anything to lengthen the time she could hope to spend alone with Belle before she dropped her off at the house she'd so hurriedly left when Violet rushed her away. They shared so much common history, their ages being the same. Though Belle, as Belle charmingly put it, had "served her time in the patriarchy" (*her words, Dillworth!*) as a married mother of two daughters.

"Well, now — you realize, Poppy — I would have to be a complete dunderhead not to know that all you women are lesbians."

Hoo boy.

"Ah, well . . ." Poppy fumbled, her heart beating suddenly faster.

"I've known about Vi since she was a girl. She loved Nan so. All these years. So faithful, even when Nan ran around on her, a new affair every year or so . . . but, Vi always hoped for the happy ending. And this is definitely not it. No. I used to tell her — Vi, there are other women in Texas, you know. Why don't you look around, honey? But she never did, just closed herself up with those moldy old movies and vegetated."

Poppy caught herself straying over the line as she watched Belle in the mirror. *C'mon, Dillworth! Let's keep this heap on the road.*

Poppy thought she caught a little hint of amusement in Belle's voice as she continued. "That's not *my* cuppa tea, nosiree. I've got twenty, maybe twenty-five years of life left to me if I take good care of myself, and I'm going to fill those years up with living. I followed the rules, just like you did, Poppy,

sitting at your typewriter in the sheriff's office —
only I did it at home, in bed, at P.T.A., at cheerleader
practice, in the kitchen. And if my girls think I'm
going to spend my freedom babysitting the grandkids!
Well!" Belle sputtered, her obvious anger growing as
she warmed to her litany of if-they-thinks.

"Yeah . . . Belle." *Oh yes, say her name.* "We
seem to've come to the same place in life — just got
here by different routes."

"Exactly."

Does that mean?

"By all lights, I've had what the world calls a
good life. Sherman was a good man and treated me
well, but he never talked to me. Never listened either.
I don't think he ever knew who I really was. He
always just chuckled and hugged me and called me
his wild woman, like any of the things that were
really important to me were simply female
aberrations."

"I know what you mean, Belle. Except that my
life with Irma was just about perfect. If I hadn't had
her I could never have faced *all* those years of
slavery. Somehow it made it bearable. But, now she's
gone and so's that hateful job . . . so it seems like
sometimes I'm a balloon cut loose to float free.
Nothing to anchor me down but nothing to hold on
to either." Poppy sucked in her lip at the end of
what seemed like an awfully long speech.

Belle placed her warm hand over Poppy's arm.
"Oh, honey — I know *just* how you feel."

I betcha my next retirement check you don't!
"Uh . . . thanks for the moral support," Poppy
managed to say as she tried hard to remember the
last time she'd *had* any feelings exactly like the ones

63

she was dealing with just now. Pit of the stomach zingers — back of the knee willies — definite below the waist excitement. And come to think of it, she had become very conscious of the roughness of her bra against her breasts.

Though sex was always good with Irma, their lovemaking had become routine and lacking in imagination as the years passed. Comfortable and satisfying . . . but not *electric* any more.

Poppy became aware that Belle had left her hand on Poppy's arm a few heartbeats longer than pure sympathy would dictate. She downshifted as the traffic slowed again, thankful for something physical to occupy her. Then Belle dropped a bomb on her.

"Oh — my support may not be all that moral. I've entertained thoughts off and on for years about what my life would be like if I was free to make other choices. Well, I'm free now — and I've been waiting a long time to meet someone like you, Poppy." Belle's clear strong voice did not hesitate as she went on. "All my life, either other folks have told me no, or I said no to myself. From here on out, I don't intend to say no to *anything*. Especially not to something that falls into the category of fun *and* low cholesterol." Belle stopped for breath. "And besides, Poppy, I think you are a very attractive woman."

Poppy felt her neck heat up.

"I didn't mean to embarrass you, Poppy. I just don't have time to waste pussyfooting around while you try to figure out what I'm all about. And while we're on that subject — I'd like to go with you to the club where you'll be meeting your private investigator friend, T.J. You can take me by my house later and help me gather up a few things, I could use the help. Besides I've never been to a women's bar."

Actually, pussyfooting wasn't too far off the truth, was it, Wondercrone?

"Um, sure. We could do that. That'd be fine."
Words often have more than one syllable, Dillworth. The woman is interested. Suck it up, girl, talk intelligent!

Poppy was sure her ears were verging on the purply crimson brilliance of a true vascular flush. She scrambled all systems and managed to take a couple of deep calming breaths before she glanced at Belle's reflection in the mirror. Brown eyes to die for were looking directly at her in that small glass rectangle. Eyes with a thousand questions and maybe a few answers. Poppy found her courage, loosened her grip on the steering wheel, grasped Belle's small hand in hers and squeezed reassuringly.

The brief but powerful connection sent a relaxing message to the tense muscles in her neck and shoulders. Warm, alive, comforting . . . empowering. She smiled then at the beautiful face in the mirror — the woman-face like hers, with wrinkles and soft folds of neck skin and bifocals and downy white fuzz on the upper lip. A sense of hopeful happiness filled her chest as Belle returned the pressure on her hand and sent a brilliant mirror smile back at her.

The wheel claimed both Poppy's hands and all her skillful attention as the traffic funneled into the rushing canyon of the North Central Expressway. The Dallas signature glass buildings grew taller and sparkled brighter on either side of them as the freeway exits forked in closer and closer together.

Adrenaline and a long-dormant, pulsing awareness

pervaded Poppy's tired body, relieving the stiffness in her knees that driving always brought. The R.V. exited the freeway, turned onto a side street and remained on it for a brief moment. Then Poppy pulled into a parking place conveniently open beside a large black van, the back end of which was equipped with a wrought-iron extension like a porch, replete with closed-up lawn chair, over which rested a neatly furled purple-and-white-striped awning. A magnetic sign on the side read *T.J.'s Home Therapy Service.* Poppy smiled at the surprisingly well-painted picture of a duck swimming beside a frog sitting on a lily-pad.

Poppy leaned close to the van as they walked toward the door of Mama Moon's and tapped her finger against the small blister window in the side of the vehicle just behind the driver's seat. A high shriek of amazing intensity answered her tapping. Belle stepped back in surprise as Poppy laughed and said, "That's Pecker. T.J.'s friend and housemate. She looks like a cockatiel but don't let that fool you. She's really a falcon in drag!"

"Well, I'm certainly glad Cleo insisted on staying at the ranch with Violet."

Poppy patted Belle's shoulder and asked, "You sure you're ready for all this?" She gestured vaguely at the van and the front of the club they were about to enter.

Belle squared her shoulders and turned her brown eyes up at Poppy. They zapped and sparkled with excitement as she nodded emphatically. "Uh-huh." She looped her arm through Poppy's. "Lead on, Papillon."

* * * * *

Poppy opened the door. Goosebumps that had nothing to do with the coolness of the afternoon xylophoned down her spine. She knew she was grinning like a baby butch in her first pair of dingo boots, but she couldn't stop. Her ears felt like they were higher than usual and her upper lip kept saying excuse me to her teeth.

She steered Belle toward a table where a very short young woman rose to greet them. It always surprised Poppy that T.J. could give the impression of height at only four feet-ten inches, but she could. Dressed as usual in the crisp, professional lab-tech whites she maintained gave her customers a sense of well-being, T.J. appraised Belle quickly. Poppy knew she had assessed exactly the nature of the intrigue between the two older women.

"May I?" With the fluid grace and physical power born of many hours at the weight bench, she pulled out a chair for Belle. Having settled her in it, she effortlessly scooted both Belle and the chair up to the table as if it were no task at all, then turned to Poppy and offered her hand. "How've you been, Pops? Good to hear from you again. I've missed you." Her pleasantly raspy June Allison voice came at them low and throaty.

Poppy braced herself for the crunch of T.J.'s handshake. The girl just didn't know her own strength.

"Still in the massage therapy business, I see," Poppy said as she rubbed the knuckles of her just freed hand.

"Yeah," T.J. answered as she ran her square hand through her blonde flattop and grinned. "Lotsa needy women out there deserve to feel better. My charter, guess you'd say. Ha, ha." Again the distinctly gruff voice that hovered around the low registers just above laryngitis, undeniably a treat to the ear. Always made Poppy want to hear it again. A woman would have to be *dead* not to respond to that voice and those hands. Poppy nodded toward Belle, who sat patiently waiting to be introduced. "Belle Stoner, meet T.J. Ballew."

T.J. rose again, took Belle's hand in hers and put it gently to her lips. "Very pleased to make your acquaintance, Ms. Stoner," she said and raised her left eyebrow eloquently at Poppy as she resumed her seat. "Okay, Pops — what's this job you want me to do?"

Poppy drew a photograph from her sweater pocket. "Seen her around?"

"Oh yeah. Blew in here from L.A. a few months back. Boogied a bit at first, then set her hooks in Nan Hightower and dropped out of sight, except for hanging out a bit with the rads over at the Women's Shelter. She calls herself Morgana, but she acts more like Pandora."

"That's her, all right." Poppy tucked the picture back into her pocket. "I want the whole scoop on her. California *and* Texas. A complete file — especially any other love interests she might have had since she and Nan became an item."

T.J. leaned forward, her scant bosom fitting beneath the table edge as she scooted in close. "This have anything to do with Nan's so-called suicide?"

Poppy looked downward at her friend, unblinking. "Yeppers — it sure does. And I need your answers

ASAP. You can reach me at this number." She wrote Zoe's phone number on the back of her business card and pushed it across the table.

T.J. raised off her chair enough to remove her wallet from a hip pocket, then extracted a card of her own for Poppy. "How you like *my* new card, Pops?"

The top of the card read *T.J. Ballew, Massage Therapy In The Comfort And Privacy Of Your Own Home.* The bottom half was covered with a repetition of the duck and frog from the side of the van, only now with little cartoon balloons over their heads. The duck said *Ducky Rubber!* and the frog said *Rubbit?*

Poppy grinned and poked at T.J.'s shoulder. "You're a case, girl."

"Well, it's an age of specialization, you know," T.J. answered, chuckling low in her throat as she reached for Poppy's card that still lay on the table.

Belle beat her to it and added a number below Zoe's. "We'll be at the ranch tomorrow by noon, but we'll be here . . . a my house, tonight." She tapped the pencil against the number she'd written on the card and raised mischievous eyes at Poppy.

Whoa-up! Bomb number two — ground zero! Take cover!

Poppy put her hand over Belle's and smiled what she fervently hoped was her very best blue-eyed, adventurous-lesbian grin.

* * * * *

Two hours later, after a marvelous meal of clam chowder and steamed vegetables at the Neighborhood Cafeteria, Poppy waited — apprehensive but excited — as Belle opened the front door of a small but well cared for English-style cottage located about six blocks from the Southern Methodist University campus. She followed her new friend inside, away from the already chilling evening air.

"The TV and VCR are in here." Belle pointed at a wide archway. "Go on and set it all up to view the tape you brought from the ranch. I know you're antsy to see it. Go on." She shooed Poppy out of the hallway. "I'll be in there in a moment to lay a fire and keep you company. But, don't start without me. I want to see it too."

All right! A fire! A beautiful woman who wants to be with me! A leprechaun in Poppy's heart danced a mad jig from atrium to ventricle and back again.

She nodded and walked through the indicated archway into a cozy living room furnished with comfortable antiques. Warm oranges and deep reds dominated the walls and coffee tables. A wide-screen television was centered in a far wall of dark wood bookcases. At the end of the room, a red brick fireplace beckoned visitors to warm themselves while they reclined on an honest-to-god bearskin rug. The bear's open mouth yawned up at Poppy where she stood frozen between the fireplace and the television. The sound of Belle's footsteps propelled her toward the bookcases.

Belle had changed into black velour harem pants and a high-collared, tight-waisted lounging jacket the color of ripe plums. The long white braid was now secured at the tip by a wide, orange-beaded band. The leprechaun in Poppy's chest clicked his heels and hopped in quick little one legged up-and-overs against her ribs. Her body responded warmly to her thoughts as she watched Belle mound cedar shavings, lay kindling, and make a fire.

Belle's hair shone that sparkly white which can only come from hair that had been, in youth, as blue-black as a raven's wing. Poppy longed to see it loosened from the braid, flowing free across the purple of her dark jacket. She imagined how good it would feel to touch a woman with desire again. With lust.

Belle rose from the hearth, walked slowly across the room and switched off the lights. The glow of the flames lit the room with soft flickering light. Belle came to stand in front of Poppy and gently took the tape box from her fingers. She laid it on the coffee table and tugged gently on Poppy's hands as she walked backward until they both stood in the center of the fur rug.

"All my life I've wondered how I would feel when this finally happened to me. But, in all my imaginings — I was never the seducer. Life is indeed perverse, Papillon." Belle encircled Poppy with her arms and tilted her eyes up to look deep into the farthest places of Poppy's soul.

Lust, need, love, tenderness, gratitude, greed — all pieced a crazy quilt of brilliant light behind Poppy's eyes as she pressed her lips gently against Belle's. *Oh, sweet . . . sweet.*

Poppy re-membered her self then. A rush of aggressive longing filled her body with heated hunger as she lowered herself to rest on her knees on the bearskin. Knees that tomorrow would carp of cautionless behavior, but now felt strong as young *bois d'arc* saplings beneath her.

Poppy pulled Belle down with her and arranged

Belle's willing body beneath hers. She covered her mouth with kisses and covered Belle's slight body with the warmth and pressure of her own larger one.

She became suddenly aware that Belle had stopped moving — in fact was tensely still. She raised herself on one elbow and looked down at her, trying to read her expression. Belle began to tremble and Poppy saw her cheeks were wet.

"Oh, Belle. What's the matter? I'm so sorry. It's been so long, I didn't mean —"

Belle put her fingers over Poppy's mouth, cutting off her apologies. "Nothing's the matter. Except there are too many clothes between us and our glasses are taking a beating." She reached up and took Poppy's glasses from her face and put them on the hearth then placed her own beside them. Then she began to unbutton Poppy's shirt.

They sat and silently undressed each other, slowly removing articles of clothing piece by piece. Poppy resisted a little the idea of completely disrobing, but Belle finally stood nude in front of Poppy and lifted her arms, displaying her body for Poppy to see. She turned slowly, cupping her breasts in her hands. "Isn't it wonderful we're the same age. We know exactly what to expect. See — no surprises."

Poppy rose then and slipped out of her slacks, peeling down her underclothes as she went. She knew her face was flaming. This little woman was outrageous. But Poppy so badly wanted to make love to Belle that it overrode her natural modesty and her sure knowledge that even though they were the same age, their bodies were not the same. Belle's was beautiful. Small, firm, milk-white breasts with dark rosebud nipples and wonderfully hollowed hipbones just exactly right to rest a cheek beside. White angel hair sparkled across her small pubic mound as she turned. Poppy sighed her approval and motioned toward the bearskin.

They lay again on the fire-warmed fur and Belle said, "Now. Again please, from the very beginning."

Poppy smiled and nodded, then remembered an unanswered question. "All right. From the beginning, but please — tell me first, why were you crying? Did I do something wrong?"

"Oh, Poppy, no. It was just the sudden pain of knowing I've waited most of life away. I was crying because we aren't girls — with all the fire and energy of youth. Because of all those wasted, lonely years. Be—"

Poppy put her fingers to Belle's mouth in echo of the moment past. "Then let's not waste any of the time we have left. I think wisdom and persistence are just as good as fire and energy . . . Besides, we might surprise ourselves."

For longer than Poppy thought possible, they made love, naked on the bearskin in front of the fire. Then they went to bed and when they woke in the night for those necessary trips to the bathroom, they talked and cuddled — all powdered and soft — and slept in each other's arms.

The next morning was one of the best in Poppy's life. She was in the shower, singing her happiness to the tiled walls, when a tapping interrupted her. She slid the door back and there stood Belle. Just Belle — no clothes, no towel — just a timid but determined smile and a now recognizable glint in her soft brown eyes.

"May I?"

73

Hooboy.

Poppy gulped, then grinned at her through the steam. "C'mon in, the water's fine."

Poppy forgot she even had knees until after breakfast when she put Sherman's big fluffy terry-cloth bathrobe in the hamper and dressed in the clean things Belle brought her. The soft corduroy pants that had belonged to Belle's oldest daughter were an exact fit. She tucked in the tail of Sherman's tan flannel shirt and adjusted the collar, resisting the urge to flip it up Elvis-style.

She sat on the edge of the bed to pull on fuzzy warm socks. *Ohmygod! Whoooeee! What the blue hell did you do to these knees, you old fool?* She rubbed both of them vigorously to relieve the sharp pain and reviewed in detail, smiling wider and wider, recalling what she had done to them. She spoke aloud to her inner self. "Might's well get a big tube of Bengay, 'cause I ain't fixing to quit doing it!"

Belle leaned her head in the doorway. "We still have to view that tape, Poppy."

A few minutes later Poppy sat on the sofa trying to concentrate on the images moving across the screen. Belle was curled up against her side, holding warmly onto the hand that Poppy had draped around her shoulder. She uncurled Poppy's fingers and pressed them against her breast. Poppy sighed and let her fingers appreciate Belle's small bosom.

They watched attentively as Zoe and Marcie re-enacted the murder. The close-ups of the ground, the zoom shots of the horizon and the area where they had parked the jeep. Belle asked a few intelligent questions and Poppy answered them as she began to access that problem-solving part of her

74

mind, that knack she'd had all those years for coming up with right answers.

She pointed the remote control module at the television, preparing to turn it off, when the footage Marcie had shot of the Drake place began to play. The scene jerked and bobbed a little, but Marcie was learning. The house and outbuildings appeared larger and larger as Marcie had used the close-up function. An outsized crow flapped into the air from its perch on a fence post just before Collin Drake appeared on the scene. His face didn't look very friendly when he turned once and glared at the camera, then stalked through the back door and into the house.

The crow, now off camera, cawed loudly on the sound track.

"Old Shapeshifter's making us listen to her," Belle said, as the tape ended and the television buzzed with static.

"Hunh?" Poppy asked as she rewound the tape. "Shapeshifter? You mean the crow?"

"Yes. It did sound ominous, didn't it? Kind of like a warning or something."

Yes. Something about the crow had bothered Poppy, too, though she couldn't put her finger on it. But she would. And when she did, she would wonder that it took her so long to see what she saw instead of what she thought she saw.

– 7 –
Meanwhile . . .
Back At The Ranch

Zoe's bright kitchen hummed with excitement as the four women sat talking around the table later that same day. Poppy squirmed as Cleo wound around her ankles and caressed the underside of her knees with the tip of her tail as she occasionally changed the direction of her circular journey. Poppy noted the dynamics above the table with a kind of elated resignation and decided that she had probably lost a partner and gained a *partner* all in the space of one night.

Marcie glowed with the obvious effects of a lesbian encounter of the first kind. If Marcie had not been hanging on Zoe's every word and expression, she would probably have noticed the exchange of sparking energy between Poppy and Belle.

But Zoe noticed.

And Poppy noticed she noticed.

They silently agreed not to notice out loud.

Poppy listened intently as Marcie recounted the events of yesterday when she and Zoe had gone to interview Coleeta Drake. "Ditsy Bitsy, *really!*" Marcie commented, with eyebrows lifted and eyes wide. "I'll never understand why anyone would choose to live alone." Big brown eyes flickered in Zoe's direction and met with the same incredulous agreement mirrored in older, wiser eyes of deceptively innocent blue.

Poppy silently registered an opinion. *Hmmm. Looks like our cowgirl has been lassoed.*

Marcie continued. "She lives in that spooky studio with all those figures standing around like real people. I bet she talks to them, too."

Zoe added her comments. "Marcie's not exaggerating, Pops. You ought to see the place. I've seen those trucks come in and out of there for years but I never really saw what they were loading up." She ran her hand through her glistening thatch of blonde hair, partly for emphasis but mostly for Marcie's benefit, Poppy thought. Either way, it was certainly fetchingly effective.

Zoe continued, "See Pops — she makes life-size

figures for museums. Not wax, but porcelain hands and heads. Then she dresses them in real clothes like Madame Tussaud's Wax Museum. She told us we just missed seeing the figure of Custer 'losing his pretty yellow hair' that the truck from Montana picked up for a museum in Billings."

Marcie began where Zoe stopped. "She's really weird, Poppy. Kept fluttering around dusting off those 'people' with an old duster that had maybe three feathers left in it. She seemed agitated, too. Her cheeks were kind of bright. Like someone with a fever. Coulda been rouge but I don't think so."

Zoe chimed in. "We were just getting around to asking her about the important stuff, like if she had ever heard from Nan's brother, J.C. Junior, since he left, when Bitsy's daddy, Collin, comes bustin' in. He just about threw us out on our butts. Said we weren't to come back any more." Zoe stopped and glanced at Marcie. "We left, but Bitsy had already told us something kind of interesting before he got there. She said she had told Nan all this before, then today — she said, 'Just today — again — I told that blonde woman in the purple pajamas the same thing. I know where J.C. is but I'm not telling because he would be verrr-ry angry at me.'"

Marcie continued the story. "Well anyway, Collin rushed us out of there and said if we came back he would call Sheriff Swindell, not that queer-loving Bubba either, he said, and have us put in jail for trespassing and performing unnatural acts in public!"

Zoe took her turn. "I guess I must've looked pretty surprised because he said, 'I saw you over there by the windmill kissing each other and there's no use denying it!' Well, what could I say? It was true, we were kissing, but I was so surprised at his outburst I couldn't think of anything to say."

Marcie spoke, her eyes wide at the memory. "I was scared, Poppy. We just got out of there as quick as possible."

Zoe leaned close to Marcie and put a protective arm around her shoulders. "Don't worry, hon. I'll take care of you."

Humph. Not only lassoed, but throwed, tied and stood over. Poppy felt her face heat up a little as her inner voice prompted a mental flash of Belle's bare breasts and brown eyes and long white hair against the bearskin rug. *Lotsa that stuff goin' around, you narrow-minded old toot!*

"Harumph." Poppy cleared her throat and shifted in her chair under sudden scrutiny from Belle, whose warm smile and sparkling eyes indicated some sort of similar mental journey. "Umm." Poppy tapped a pencil on the table as much to redirect her own thoughts as to gain control of the moment. "Speaking of my little buddy, Bubba, we need to see him about some things in that so-called report he smuggled to me. The forensics data on the pistol type and shots fired and all that wasn't in it." Poppy fell silent, then mused out loud. "Wonder how Morgana of the purple P.J.'s took Bitsy's news about the whereabouts of Nan's brother and his million-dollar scrotum?"

Not waiting for an answer, Poppy spoke to Marcie but glanced at Zoe as well. "You two seem to be working well as a team. Except for public displays of affection." She grinned at Marcie's quick blush and continued. "Zoe — that's private property down there at that old homestead. You can tell Collin Drake that if you have any more trouble out of him. And if he

79

shoots his ugly mouth off about what folks do in private, tell him you'll have him arrested for a peeping tom."

Poppy waited as the relieved laughter died down, then she said, "And seein's how Lupe is taking care of Violet up at the big house, I'm going to try to talk Belle into turning her hand at the 'Watson' business."

Belle took Poppy's hand and raised it to her lips for a quick but unmistakable kiss. "I don't think it'll take much persuasion, my dear Papillon. You'll have to pry me away from your side after last night."

Poppy felt the leprechaun keeping time in her chest, poking his little shillelagh against her ribs. *It's probably just happiness, Wondercrone. Don't go for the Digitalis yet!*

Marcie finally figured it out. Her mouth fell open in surprise as Belle released Poppy's hand and then primly sat back in her chair and stroked Cleo who had appeared in her lap.

"But, what —" Marcie began.

"But what, *what*, Sugarpie? I'll tell if you will."

Cleo's bubbly purr was the only sound in the room as Marcie closed her mouth tightly shut and blushed so hard she could pass for sunburnt.

— 8 —

The Valley Girl Checks Out

After lunch Poppy dispatched Marcie and Zoe to take care of getting the forensics report from Bubba. Then she and Belle and, of course, Cleo, drove up to the guest house to interview Morgana. The cold clear weather had held and the golden afternoon sun slanted across the hills, sharpening the winter scene with hard-lined shadows like those in a Van Gogh landscape.

Poppy expertly guided the small R.V. over the

rocky ranch roads. The recent rains had washed some of the dirt away from the low places where the road wound up and around the red hills.

Belle startled Poppy by suddenly speaking after a long quiet moment. "Stop, Poppy. Look!" She pointed across Poppy's chest out the side window.

A buck and three does had been grazing and now stood completely still, outlined sharply against the brilliant blue sky, warily watching their watchers.

"Aren't they beautiful?" Belle sighed, and turned her head to follow their flight as they made their decision to run, bounding through the tall yellowed grass and across the road a few yards in front of them. Cleo stood on Belle's thigh, front paws against the window, and watched them also.

"Yep. They sure are." Poppy had sighted them through the cross-hairs of a mental scope and tasted fresh venison so smartly that saliva had spurted from under her tongue, but she thought it unwise to make Belle aware of any of this . . . yet. There obviously were things she must learn about this woman who sat beside her. This woman who made her feel alive again. Who in so short a time had become a Significant Other in Poppy's life.

The guest house loomed in the clearing just as they topped the last hill before the land fell away to the river bottoms. The weathered gray of the natural cedar wood complemented the native stone of the lower part of the house. A wide deck enclosed the dwelling on three sides, while a large garage flanked it on the near side.

A cardinal flashed crimson against the gray house as they pulled into the drive beside Morgana's garish lavender VW. Poppy thought it odd there was no smoke coming from the chimney. She scanned the woodpile and quickly noted a plentiful supply of cordwood. *That California gal probably doesn't know how to make a fire. Got the electric heaters cranked up to meltdown level, I betcha.*

A fence constructed of ancient weathered fenceposts, stacked together in a criss-cross pattern, snaked its way loosely around the lower cactus gardens. The path to the front door was laid with large, dark red fossil rocks, clearly marked with the spiral casts of shells. Poppy's radar began to buzz a warning to her. She stopped abruptly and Belle bumped into her. "Something's wrong. Stay close behind me." She pulled her small .38 from her pocket, holster and all, unsnapped the leather flap from across the hammer and slipped the snub-nosed revolver free. She felt Belle tense behind her at the sound of the tiny click that signified she had the pistol cocked and ready to fire.

Poppy knocked loudly, waited a moment. No answer. She knocked again. Louder. Still no sound from the other side of the door. Except for a bubbly, somehow familiar hum that sounded louder to Poppy as the silence deepened around them.

She pulled on her glove and tried to turn the door knob. "It's locked. Let's see if it's locked up all the way around." She motioned with her gun hand for Belle to follow and moved slowly, carefully, past the front windows to the corner of the deck. They threaded their way between wrought-iron chairs and around a table with its colorful umbrella furled, to a doorway beside a barbecue pit.

"It's locked too," Poppy said.

They made their way quickly along a fireplace

wall, unbroken by windows, past more chairs and tables. Poppy peeked cautiously around the corner at the back door. Nothing out of place on the back deck, but nothing moving either.

She thumped the door hard, but no one stirred inside. Except the humming seemed more audible. "Damn. This one's locked, too." She turned to Belle. "What the hell is that funny noise?"

"I don't know. It sounds like an aquarium or something." Cleo's ears twitched, as if she too, were trying to identify the sound.

"Well, hell, Belle," Poppy said, completely unaware of her unplanned rhyme. "You're almost right. It's the hot tub! She's got the Jacuzzi going in the hot tub." She looked sheepishly at the cocked pistol in her hand and pointed it at the floor as she carefully lowered the hammer and reset the safety. She looked around the end of the deck at a fogged up window that was raised a couple of inches. Steam oozed from it slowly into the outside air.

"That must be the bathroom window. I'll go tap on it. Hope I don't scare the girl to death." *You better hope she's in there alone and not doing something kinky with the bubble machine, Fearless Tracker!*

"Wait here a minute, hon," Poppy cautioned to Belle, who clutched the omnipresent Cleo to her chest. Then she climbed down the deck steps and walked to the window closest to the corner where the back of the garage right-angled away from the house. She found a piece of unused lattice strip and pecked on the glass. "Hey. Morgana! . . . You in there? . . . Yoohoo!"

When you gonna learn to listen to your own intuition, Dillworth? You don't see any good-looking blonde appearing up there, do you? She looked back at Belle, earnestly worried now.

"Something's really wrong in there, isn't it?" Belle asked.

"Don't know yet. Might be." Poppy walked toward a gardening shed for the ladder leaning against it. "Come help me get this up against the house, then hold it steady while I go up and see."

Cleo escaped Belle's arms, leaped nimbly to the deck railing and seemed to watch the two women with apprehension as they dragged the aluminum ladder across the yard and leaned it up against the side of the house.

Poppy's heart thumped as she climbed toward the opening where tendrils of steam wafted out, curling down and then up into the cold air.

At first she thought everything was all right. A flash of naked body moved against the deep maroon side of the large sculptured tub. Poppy sucked in air to holler, then let it out slowly as she realized Morgana's movements were unnatural.

The action of the Jacuzzi was pushing her stiffened body in lazy circles, bumping her head against the tub. She floated on her back, her hair billowing Medusa-like around her face. Suddenly the swirling action of the water sucked Morgana's head under and Poppy jerked in surprise, almost losing her footing on the ladder.

No doubt about it. The woman was dead. Had been for some time. Just about parboiled. Hot water had been trickling in a tiny stream from the faucet,

85

just enough to keep the tub filled. Poppy turned her head from the window to fill her lungs with cold air that didn't smell like something cooking.

She backed carefully down the ladder and tried not to let the horror show in her eyes, but didn't quite make it. She wanted to sit down — or maybe vomit. Instead she ducked her head against Belle's neck and hugged her hard until the nausea passed.

"She's dead, Belle. Drowned. Or something."

Belle, shocked but fairly calm, reclaimed her skittish cat and they hurried back to the R.V. and climbed in. "Let's get back to Zoe's and call Bubba Swindell."

– 9 –
By the Numbers

A few hectic hours later Poppy stood against the deck railing of Morgana's house and looked into the distance. The shortness of December days was obvious in the purpling shadows down along the river. Just across the fence from the homestead place, smoke rose lazily from the kilns at Coleeta Drake's studio. Though it was cold, there was no wind at all. A change was due soon. Poppy could feel it in her bones. Her thoughts piled up like folders labeled *work to be done.*

She mentally tagged each event and sorted it into its place among the others of the puzzle she was trying to solve. She was only dimly aware of Belle draping a jacket around her shoulders.

Bubba had come promptly in his shiny black 'Vader Wagon,' as Zoe called it, and efficiently examined the house, supervised removal of Morgana's body and closed the place up with a yellow tape over the front door marked NO ADMITTANCE — CRIME SCENE.

It appeared that someone had hit Morgana over the head with one of the heavy stone-butted cigarette lighters, and then she had either drowned in the tub or had been drowned by that same somebody. The business with the hot water was either just plain macabre or very shrewd.

At first blush it looked bad for Violet. Poppy hoped she had a firm alibi for whatever the time of death turned out to be. But that might be hard to determine because the body wouldn't have cooled at a normal rate. The oversized hot water heater, evidently installed with hot-tub use in mind, had been almost emptied of heated water by the constant thin stream coming from the faucet.

Poppy turned her attention toward the jeep where Zoe, Marcie and Belle waited. She mentally agreed again with Zoe's earlier expression of relief that Bubba's father and the rest of the clowns were busy at the gravel pit showing off the body parts they'd quarried to the TV reporters from the city. And so, thankfully, they were not on hand to mess up this murder scene as they'd done when Nan died.

Poppy slipped her arms into the sleeves of her jacket and joined the others in the jeep. They were quiet on the way back to Zoe's cabin. Poppy remembered the report Bubba had just given her on the pistol Nan had been killed with. She looked at it in the failing light and took off her glasses, cleaned them, then held the paper up and squinted hard to read something. "Is that word *three?* Does it say the pistol had been fired *three* times?"

Zoe handed a flashlight over her shoulder to Belle who shined it on the paper and verified it was indeed *three.*

"Hmmm," Poppy mused. "Well, how about that? Look here, Belle." Poppy tapped the paper with a thumbnail. "It says here that one shot was fired approximately twenty years ago and the other two shots very recently."

Poppy folded the paper excitedly and put it in her pocket. "That old .45 revolver belonged to Nan's father, didn't it, Zoe? Wasn't it the one he supposedly carried during World War Two? And *his* daddy fought the Huns with it in the first big war? The same pistol Lupe said had been lost or stolen for years, right? Until it showed up beside Nan's body?"

Poppy could feel her level of excitement rise until she was almost bouncing on the edge of her seat. She had that special feeling. She *knew* this was a significant part of the puzzle.

One shot, long ago for who knows what . . . then another one for what reason? And the third that killed Nan. Had J.C. stolen the pistol? Had he killed Nan? And if he did, then why kill Morgana, his only means of apparent gain?

It would come. The answer would come. She knew it would.

Zoe had answered Poppy's earlier question about the pistol affirmatively, but Poppy's attention had turned inward, mentally stacking, shuffling and restacking all those labeled folders. Something important was missing from the order. An empty, flat folder stuck out, counter to the others, in that imaginary sequence-of-events file.

When they arrived at the house the phone was ringing. Zoe raced to catch it. "Yes . . . no! Ohmygod! Are *you* okay?" She turned to look worriedly at Belle. "All right, I'll tell her, Lupe, but she'd not gonna like it." She cradled the phone and said slowly, "Belle, Lupe says the sheriff just left. Violet's been arrested for Morgana's murder. Bubba found her fingerprints on the murder weapon."

Belle squeezed Poppy's hand, then released it and dug in her purse for a moment before extracting a small blue address book. She went unhesitatingly to the phone and rapidly punched a series of numbers.

"Yes, you *may* help me." She spoke firmly into the receiver. "Tell Cletus Barns to meet Belle Stoner at the Rojo county jail in one hour. Violet Cooper has been arrested for murder . . . I don't care if he *is* at Lake Texoma. That's all the better. Tell him to get that whirlybird in the air *muy pronto*. If I don't see his fancy whale-belly boots coming through that door within the hour, you can tell him to forget all about making his next few years' worth of Neiman's payments!"

Belle drew a long breath and nodded as she evidently listened to someone repeat instructions. "That's right. One hour from now. Thank you, dear."

She decisively placed the phone receiver in the cradle and turned to Poppy. "Now. Let's go pick up Lupe and see about getting that poor child out of jail."

Poppy was all set to herd everyone out the door when a loud knock sounded.

Zoe opened the door to reveal Rick, Zoe's second-in-command ranch boss, standing on the stoop with his hat in his hand. "May I talk to you folks a few minutes? I had to tell Bubba Swindell some things I think you oughta know about."

– 10 –

Of Cowboys and Cat Burglars

Poppy closely observed the tall, handsome young man, obviously dressed for going out, who had just sat gracefully on one of Zoe's hard kitchen chairs and crossed a booted ankle over his knee. He sedately placed his wide-brimmed Stetson in his lap over the rounded bulges of his crotch.

Whooeee! Betcha he makes all the buffalo gals come out to dance!

He spoke apologetically to Belle and Zoe. "When

Bubba was here earlier, he asked me if I'd seen anyone go down toward the guest house last night or today. Well, I told him I'd seen Miss Cooper go down that way late last evening and come back a while later. I hung around until I saw her come back 'cause I thought I might have to go pull that big old Caddy of hers out of one of the creek bottoms. They're pretty rough since it rained last week."

Rick pulled a loose thread in the hem of his Levis out about two inches, then raised his pant leg above the top of his boot and extracted a Buck knife from a little scabbard just inside the pull tab. He opened the blade and sawed delicately at the offending thread as he continued to speak.

"It got to be about dark-thirty and I was just fixing to start for the tractor shed when I saw her headlights coming over the hill. I waved to her as she passed by me, but she was crying and rubbing at her eyes. She really looked awful. I don't think she saw me at all."

"You tell Bubba that part, about her crying?" Poppy asked.

"Nope. Figured he didn't need to know that part."

"You're a good friend, Ricko. Thanks," Zoe told him. "I appreciate your telling us all this. Things are kinda crazy on the ranch just now."

"Yeah — s'too bad about Morgana . . . You know, I saw that little bug of hers parked in Collin Drake's driveway yesterday afternoon as I went into town to pick up feed. What in the world you s'pose she had to say to that mean-tempered old redneck?"

Poppy answered, "I don't know, Rick. Did you tell Swindell about seeing her there?"

"Nope. He didn't ask."

Poppy stood and raised an eyebrow at Zoe who caught her drift and rose from her chair.

"Well, thanks, Rick. I reckon you're fixin' to go down to Dallas and give all those city boys a thrill, are you?"

Boys? Well, Dillworth you dingaling! O'course. The young fella's Gay. Not all of 'em decorate interiors you know!

Poppy tried not to let her chagrin show on her face as she noticed that Rick had blushed at Zoe's weighted teasing.

The front door had no more than closed on his exit than the phone rang. "For Poppy," Zoe announced and handed her the receiver. Poppy waved the other three women back into the room as she listened to T.J. talk excitedly.

"Yeah, Pops. Ms. Stephanie Alice Michaels, a.k.a. Morgana, was having a hot and heavy affair with one of the top women golfers on the tour. And hold onto your hat — a *married* one!"

"Jealous husband?"

"Nah. The marriage is probably one of those convenience things. But the husband's also her coach and you see them on TV all the time — huggy-kissy stuff — selling a lot of real wholesome items. Get the picture?"

"Unh-hunh."

"Okay. Here's the story as far as I can dig it out. On Halloween evening about four or five o'clock, before the crowd on Cedar Springs got to the really crazy stage, Nan Hightower came in the Knew Age jewelry store and was just about to give the clerk her credit card to pay for some earrings she'd picked out

94

when she evidently saw someone she knew pass by outside. She pocketed the earrings, left her card layin' on the counter and split, extremely agitated. She was heard to say something like 'I'll kill the lying bitch' as she went out onto the street and disappeared into the crowd."

Poppy motioned for quiet behind her as Zoe, Marcie and Belle grew restless to leave for the sheriff's office.

"She what? Speak up, T.J."

"Clerk says Nan was dressed all in black like a cat burglar and she was wearing a cat mask. After the store closed, Beth — the clerk — says she looked for Nan off and on to tell her about her card. She saw her out on the street in the throng of crazies about eleven o'clock but lost her as the parade moved on by."

"Yeah . . . well?" Poppy prompted impatiently as T.J. caught her breath.

"Okay. I'll get to the point. Seems like Nan spotted Morgana and the golfette sportin' down the street — all brazen in their spook-suits — and followed them all evening, the whole length of the parade route. She finally tracked them to a condo complex where Nan apparently took her own disguise to heart. She climbed a fence and up a tree and caught them both bare-assed naked on the balcony doin' some kind of moon ritual with a battery-op dildo."

"Jesusmaryandjoseph!"

"Yeah. Well — after a bit of delicate pressure, I found all this out from the lady golfer who, by the way, has offered to give me a free condo for life if I'll keep my mouth shut. I told her not to worry about *my* mouth. The one that'll come unhinged will be Morgana's. She —"

"Breaker-breaker, little buddy. Listen up. Morgana's dead. Murdered today, or last night. Zoe's boss has been arrested and we're on our way now to the jailhouse in Todo Rojo to see her. You did a good job, T.J. Keep your ears open. Eyes too. I got to go now. I'll call you later tonight after we see what's happening with Ms. Cooper."

"Gotcha. And good God what a mess!" T.J. rung off.

"Rodge — later." Poppy hung up and pointed at the doorway. "Let's go and pick up Lupe. I'll fill you in on the way to town."

* * * * *

As they parked by the courthouse, Belle said quietly, "Poor, poor Nan. She must've been just about destroyed to find Morgana like that. After changing her will and wanting a *child* from that foolish girl."

Poppy patted Belle's hand and felt admiration rise inside her for this little woman who could calmly demand immediate action from one of Dallas' most formidable attorneys and still have compassion in her heart for a philandering dead woman.

Some gal, Dillworth. A helluva lot more'n you bargained for. Irma woulda liked her, ya know.

Marcie spoke for the first time in a while. "Except for the fact that Morgana's dead, she'd be about the best suspect in Nan's murder."

"Besides J.C.," Zoe added, hammering her own favorite nail.

96

Poppy silently considered these points and others as the five women climbed the steps past the green soldier and through the big courthouse doors. The weather was on the move. A sudden gust of cold wind jerked the door away from Poppy's hand. Her knuckles burned against the sharp edge of the brass latch. *Shoulda worn gloves.*

Her thoughts predictably followed the track she'd just switched onto. Nan had worn gloves. That'd been one of the things the suicide ruling was based on. Nan was left-handed. Bullet entered left temple. Appropriate pattern of powder burns detected on left glove. Nan had a real thing for leather, Zoe'd said. Bought a new outfit, head to toe every year, so she could play Zorro atop that big black horse.

The hairs on the nape of Poppy's neck lifted and began the crazy little dance they did when she felt that old feeling of something about to fit together. She would ask Bubba to show her Nan's clothing. There was something . . .

The musty, familiar smell of the sheriff's office invaded Poppy's nose, yanking her thoughts to the present moment. She watched Belle calmly instruct Pappy Swindell that they would see Violet now. Poppy's eyes filled with quick tears and she swallowed back a lump at the memory of the other time she'd stood in this office, consumed with painful longing for Irma.

Now it was different. She wasn't alone anymore. She brushed angrily at the tears that threatened to escape down her cheek, fell in quickly behind Lupe and walked in the direction indicated by Belle's beckoning finger.

It was almost showtime!

What would the main feature be, *Woman In Chains*, starring Ida Lupino? *Pappy's Prisoner*, starring Loretta Young, or *A Woman in Trouble*, starring just plain Vi Cooper?

– 11 –
Matchless Violet

The five women arranged themselves in a yellow-lit hallway around the outside of a drafty, old-fashioned jail cell. Floor-to-ceiling bars ran along the front with a rust-flecked, round-barred sliding gate in the center. Violet Cooper's many-ringed fingers curled around the bars, the curving red-lacquered nails reminding Poppy of the grasping feet of a caged bird.

Belle spoke to her reassuringly. "Cletus Barnes

will be here very soon, Vi, to post bail, and then you'll be free to go back home with us."

Poppy was still waiting to see which persona they were dealing with, but so far no immediately recognizable characteristics were present. Just Violet Cooper, innocent woman, scared our of her wits by the specter of spending not only Christmas but the rest of her life behind bars.

Violet's hands were shaking. Belle took one and Lupe the other, and Poppy heard both women make appropriately comforting sounds. She moved past them and down the hall to where Pappy Swindell sat in a cane-bottom chair toying with an honest-to-god, just-like-in-the-movies ring of oversized keys.

"Highdee, Miz Dillworth. What can I do for you?" he asked as Poppy stood in front of him, loudly clearing her throat.

"I'd like to see the clothing that Nan Hightower was wearing when she died."

"Well, that shouldn't be too hard to do. Except I'll have to get John T. to show it to you, seein's how I can't leave the theater here unattended." He winked broadly up at Poppy, happy with his little joke. He poked his bent index finger in the dial of an ancient black phone and pushed it around three times.

"John T. . . . Pappy here. A lady — Miz Dillworth — is coming down there. Get the Hightower box out of the back room and show her the stuff in it . . . Well, Bert ain't here and that makes me boss!" Pappy Swindell's face reddened as his request met with obvious opposition.

"John T., you g'on ahead and do what I say or I'll make sure your mama-in-law finds out how much attention you been payin' to your ex-wife's little sister down at the V.F.W. on bingo night." The old man grinned at Poppy. "Right. She'll be down there in a minute," he told the phone.

"Y'know," he said to Poppy as he hung up the receiver. "If you punch the right buttons, you can get just about *any* job done." He slapped the key ring against his pants leg, plainly enjoying his own shrewdness.

"Pappy," Poppy began, "Why are you helping me? Your son didn't seem too interested in our poking around in the Hightower case."

"Well, t'tell the truth, I really think Bubba's got the right slant on this one. Bert don't give him enough credit. The boy's real smart, he just ain't had the chance to build up any confidence in hisself. Man who lacks confidence in hisself at work cain't command respect from others. 'Specially from his loved ones. A big old stubborn red-headed wife, for instance."

He rose creakily and stretched. "Back down those stairs to the main desk. John T.'ll help you out."

Poppy thanked the old man and hurried toward the stairs. She had to flatten herself against the wall to avoid colliding with Cletus Barnes who ascended the steps two at a time, spurred on by an emotional imperative that probably had a lot to do with making his Neiman-Marcus payments on time. She continued on her way downstairs. She had to see those clothes. Something about them was nagging at the edges of her mind.

John T.'s head sat squarely on his rounded beefy shoulders. Poppy recognized him at once as the no-neck deputy described by Zoe the day they had

101

made the video at the murder scene on the bluff. He had placed an open cardboard box on the desk in front of him for Poppy's inspection. His head dipped forward in a squinty-eyed nod and he grunted what Poppy assumed was permission for her to remove the plastic bagged items from the box.

First a new black leather jacket with various areas on the left shoulder and sleeve outlined in some kind of white marker ink. A pair of worn black leather driving gloves, the left one tagged and marked with some of the same ink. The pistol: a large revolver, obviously old but not rusty. Three .45 caliber shell casings in a baggie with three unspent bullets, each of which was cut on its lead nose with a deep X . . . a mark Poppy knew to be made by marksmen wanting the most killing power out of their shot. The soft lead would tear and curl outward from the incised lines of the X, delivering more destruction to the mass of the target when it exited.

The report had stated that considering the ammunition type and the condition of the rest of the weapon, especially the fired chambers, the bullets had been placed in the pistol probably forty to fifty years ago. Which meant Joseph Calvin Hightower, Senior, himself likely loaded the very bullet into the pistol that eventually killed his own daughter. Might have done it before she was even born.

She examined the items one by one, then returned them neatly to the box. "Thank you, Deputy," she said in the direction of John T. who had stood motionless beside the box, never wavering in his slit-eyed surveillance of Poppy's actions.

"Unh," he grunted.

Talkative fella. Probably uncomfortable without a cliff to piss off of.

Suddenly the soothing vibrato of Cletus Barnes at his golden-throated best hummed in Poppy's outer ear, taking precedence over her wry inner musings. She hurried upstairs just in time to see Swindell the Elder hanging up the phone.

"Bert says the judge is on his way down here to sign off on them papers you got there, Barnes. After that happens, then I'm to release Miz Cooper into the custody of her aunt here, Miz Stoner . . . But, you know she ain't to be leaving the county before the trial." He inclined his shock of white hair in the general direction of Violet, who now stood calmly in her cell.

Looking back at the rather disheveled lawyer, Pappy Swindell grinned at his audience then spoke directly to Barnes. "Bert says you just set some kinda speed record gettin' here from your cabin in Texoma and to be sure to give you a Kleenex so's you can clean the bugs off your teeth. Hee hee!"

Poppy held back a smile as Barnes reddened and removed his glasses for a proper cleaning of each lens.

The next half-hour was filled with hectic activity as the promised judge arrived, papers were signed and Violet was released.

Soon they were outside, huddling against the cold wind, stuffing themselves into the small jeep like teenagers on a hay ride. Poppy didn't mind the inconvenience at all as she cuddled Belle on her lap for the ride back to the ranch. *Knees? What knees?*

Violet sat beside Poppy in the middle of the back

seat with Lupe on the other side of Violet by the windows, while Zoe drove and Marcie amply filled the other front bucket seat.

Poppy was glad for the chance to ask Violet a few questions. "Miz Cooper, if I —"

"You may call me Violet. Ms. Cooper sounds a little formal in light of our current situation." She smiled indulgently at Poppy, then at her Aunt Belle who had melted comfortably into the circle of Poppy's protecting arms. "Especially as you seem to have captured the heart of my only living relative."

"Shame on you, Vi Cooper," Belle retorted. "You have other living relatives. But that's beside the point. You're absolutely right about my heart belonging to Papillon. Except it wasn't captured — I gave it freely."

As this was Poppy's first time to hear this declaration, tears quickened at the corners of her eyes. She struggled against their escape and subsequent betrayal of the depth of her emotion. She reeled inwardly at the surprising discovery that she had not dared to dream that something so wonderful as *future* with Bell might be a possibility.

Poppy cleared her throat but her voice was still a bit husky with emotion when she spoke. "Thank you, Belle." What could she say on such short notice? How to respond to a gift of such magnitude? Well, Belle had told her she didn't have time to pussyfoot around, but this was mighty quick indeed.

Poppy hugged Belle tighter and tried to concentrate on the questions she needed to ask Violet. But that was extremely difficult. The unaccustomed physical reaction of her own body to the warmth and friction of Belle on her lap was on the verge of shutting down the possibility of making mental deductions. Brilliant or otherwise.

"Violet," Poppy began. "There are a few points I think you can clear up for me, if you will."

There was little room for dramatics, but Violet managed to do a pretty fair shoulders-up, chin-out Crawford Under Fire. "I will answer all of your questions, but first I must have a bit of time by myself. This whole experience has been extremely unnerving. If it's not too much trouble, could you come to my sitting room in about an hour?"

"Well . . . sure. Sure, I could do that," Poppy answered. *Maybe something above the waist will be working by then, Dillworth. We're skirting mighty close to damp underwear here.*

*   *   *   *   *

At the appointed hour, Poppy stood waiting with Belle in the large room where Barnes had read the will. Cleo leaped from a chair to the long low mantle over which hung a row of framed photographs. Poppy picked out the pistol right away. Its first appearance was in the holster of a mustachioed man on a horse. The sepia print was old and faded but it was clearly the same pistol she had just seen in town.

She absently stroked Cleo's back as the hedonistic cat pranced back and forth in front of her. The next time she saw the pistol, it was pushed rakishly into the belt of a young doughboy who stood with a group of boyish soldiers next to a sign that read *Paris, 12 K.*

Its next appearance was in the hands of a helmeted Marine who had to be J.C. Senior. He was

105

sighting along it, his profile pointed at a distant group of palm trees.

The last picture in the group seemed to have been added almost as an afterthought. It was smaller and the style of frame differed from the others. It was a small, black-and-white snapshot of a young boy, six or seven maybe, who was holding the huge pistol out in front of him with both hands, his face pinched into a fearful shut-eyed grimace unnoticed by his father who pointed proudly toward a homemade target some yards away. *Hmmm. Just a boy and his toy, Sherlock?* Hadn't Lupe said the gun disappeared some years back? Maybe the same time as Junior's escape to the north?

Lupe stepped into the room and announced, "Miss Violet will see you now." She turned to lead them down the hall, but Poppy took her elbow, gently stopping her.

"Lupe, do you remember exactly when the big pistol disappeared? The one in those pictures?" She gestured at the mantle.

Lupe's eyes widened as she darted a look where Poppy pointed. She brought her hands together and her already sloping shoulders drooped resignedly. "Mr. Hightower, he and Mister Junior, they had a big fight about that *pistola* the night before he disappeared, all those years ago. After that poor boy left, his daddy swear that he stole the weapon to pay for his trip to Canada." Lupe stopped talking and looked worriedly down the hallway, plainly anxious to end the conversation.

"But, what do *you* think, Lupe?" Poppy still held her arm.

"Yes . . . I think the boy took it. But, I think he

took it to throw it away. He hated weapons and killing, all his life he stayed away from that kind of thing. I think that is why he finally left this house. Because his daddy never understood. He was a very unhappy boy."

Poppy released Lupe's arm and Lupe walked rapidly away from her, rubbing her hands on the hem of her apron. Then Lupe knelt, scooped Cleo up in her arms and pressed a button beside one of a set of doors at the end of the hallway.

From the speaker over their heads came the clear tones of a woman now completely in command of all her faculties. *"Yes Lupe. Bring them into the boudoir, please."* The requested bit of time had apparently been put to good use.

Lupe opened the doors wide and Poppy and Belle followed her through the "Ali Baba" sitting room and into a huge bedroom that Poppy thought could easily have been the set for half the movies made between 1925 and 1945. A round canopied bed, plumped and dimpled and draped with tuck-and-button white satin, filled one end of the room. Two sixteenth-century armoires flanked an arched doorway where beads still swung lightly as if someone had just passed through them.

Poppy sensed the bead-swinger somewhere behind her and turned to find her intuition was right on the mark. Violet Cooper rose from her seat on the end of an Egyptian-styled chaise lounge. She walked toward her visitors, cigarette awave in one hand while the other one, stiff arm, limp wrist, jeweled fingers down, plowed through the air toward Poppy.

Who did the only dykey thing she felt was appropriate under the circumstances. She placed one hand behind her back, took the Star's extended fingers in her other hand and raised them to her lips while executing a sharp, heels together bow from the waist.

Then, slightly astonished at her own audacity, Poppy watched Violet closely and was rewarded by a quick twinkle of amusement that she supposed must be Violet's pleasure in Poppy's willingness to play the game.

Belle, however, was not having any of her niece's theatrics and barked at her in a disgusted tone, "Violet, settle down. Stop flying about and light somewhere so Poppy can ask you some questions."

Violet sent her a quick-but-fetching Shirley Temple pout, then did indeed settle herself in a fan-shaped, pink rattan seashell chair in front of a low marble table. She waved Poppy and Belle onto the pink satin cushions of two other shell chairs.

Poppy did not feel like a pearl. She felt like an idiot. But she extracted her list of questions from her hip pocket and unfolded it, smoothing the wrinkles against the cool pink marble. Before she could begin, however, Violet spoke up. "Auntie Belle, you rascal. So you've finally come around to sup at Sappho's table."

Poppy noticed that Belle blushed in spite of herself. "We're not here to discuss my sexual orientation, Vi. But, since you've brought it up, and conjured such a beautiful image at that . . ." She glanced knowingly at Poppy. "Yes. I'm here and I intend to sup at every opportunity. Now, Poppy, ask my niece what you need to know so we can get to bed."

Poppy noted that Violet barely suppressed a chuckle and did not even try to hide her enjoyment of Poppy's discomfort at Belle's last comment.

"Harumph." *Great start, Wondercrone.* "Well, first off, I'd like to know if Barnes has ever said why Nan wanted to see him the morning she was ki — she died?"

"Cletus told me Nan had mentioned wanting to make more changes in her will. She didn't tell him what, but he said *he* thought *she* thought she had probably been hasty about making the changes she had just signed and that perhaps she wanted to change them back again or strike them entirely." Violet sat back in her pink seashell, an enigmatic Anna Karenina, rivaling Garbo at her best.

Switching movies almost too quickly for Poppy to keep up, Violet exploded from the chair and stalked across the room, turn-pace-turn, still Garbo but . . . *yes! Queen Christina.*

"That's why I believe Nan killed herself. I think something happened in Dallas that Halloween weekend. Something that Nan could not live with."

She glowered at Poppy. Elbows out, hands on hips, spread legs. Toss head, turn, speak from profile —

Now who th'

Slight tremble to the chin, full face now, eyes half closed but glinting with fiery emotion.

Of course, Dillworth. Hepburn — The Lion In Winter.

"And it had something to do with Morgana. I'm sure of it. I knew Nan, remember? I . . . knew . . . her." Puff-wave-turn. Walk slowly to the chair,

109

Davis-dump the cigarette into the heavy crystal ashtray, sit and wait with folded hands for the private investigator to go on with the inquisition.

Poppy took a deep breath and began her next question. "Thank you, Violet," she said first, as much for the answer to her first question as in appreciation of the performance. "Rick told us that he saw you go down toward the guest house the night Morgana was killed. That he waited for you to come back because he feared you might get stuck somewhere and would need his help."

This one was easy. Olivia DeHavilland looked back at Poppy with Scarlett O'Hara eyes that said, *Yayus, Ah've made mistakes, but it wasn't all mah fawult. It was that awful wawuh!*

"Yes, I did go to the guest house. I went to get my drawings. The plans I've been making for years for my dream house down by the old homestead. It's been my habit to sit on the deck there and visualize on paper the house Nan and I would build someday. I couldn't leave something so personal and precious to me in the house with *that* woman!"

Belle placed a restraining, comforting hand on her niece's arm as she appeared ready to lift off into another high-energy performance.

"Did you talk to her while you were there?" Poppy asked.

"I don't know if she even knew I *was* there. I knocked but didn't get any answer, so I got the key from its regular place under the fossil rock and opened the door and went in. I heard the Jacuzzi running and assumed she was in the bathroom. I retrieved the roll of drawings from beneath the window seat in the front room, closed and locked the door — replaced the key and left."

"That shouldn't have taken much time. Rick says he waited quite a while, maybe an hour before he saw you return."

Violet sat silent, stoic. Poppy waited for the next feature to begin. *Trouble in the projection room?*

Belle urged, "This looks pretty bad for you, Violet. You had motive and opportunity, *and* your fingerprints were found on the murder weapon. You must tell Poppy everything . . . please."

The RKO searchlights faded. Reality seemed to fall like a damp cloak around Violet's shoulders. She shuddered, hugged herself and hunched forward on the edge of her chair. Just plain Violet Cooper, ready now to bare all. No matter the cost.

"All right. But there's not really much to tell. I took the drawings down to the old home place and spread them out to look at them one last time. I don't know how long I sat there by the windmill. I cried for all my dead dreams. I wanted to burn the drawings, an exercise in futility I suppose, but it's what I wanted to do. But I could *not* find a match. I'd left the house without my purse, the cigarette lighter in the car was useless. I tried, but it only made round holes in the paper. Finally I just rolled them all up again and dropped them into that old well. The one Nan's great-grandfather built back in the Indian days . . ."

Poppy waited impatiently as Violet continued. "And that's it. I came home then and went to bed."

"Well, Violet." Poppy folded her paper and put it back in her pocket. The rest of the questions were unimportant in light of this latest revelation. "We must rescue those drawings from the well. I'm sure Bubba Swindell and Cletus Barns will agree that they're evidence of why you went to the guest house after having told Morgana you never wanted to see her again."

Real tears rolled down Violet's cheeks as Belle hugged her shoulders. "Don't worry, honey. Poppy will fix everything all up," Belle crooned to her niece as she patted her arm.

Poppy gulped and thought about crumbly old wells, sheriffs, lawyers, the blue norther beginning to rattle the windows, and last-but-oh-no-not-least, how Papillon Audubon Dillworth was going to make everything all better.

– 12 –
To the Well Once Too Often

The next day dawned clear and still, the brief gusty norther having spent itself quickly. Poppy lay thinking quietly in bed, luxuriating in the unaccustomed glow of knowing another woman's sweet, warm body was snuggled against her side. Belle made occasional small *miffle* sounds from the back of her throat that might have been tiny snores. Poppy loved them. They made a giggle rise from somewhere deep in her abdomen.

No doubt about it. Her feelings for Belle had bloomed into . . . love? Extreme like? Whatever. She adored the little woman. Near the foot of the bed Cleo stirred and stretched her big white paws against Poppy's leg.

Yeppers. Even like her damn cat. Wonder how that happened?

Being a dog-person had limited Poppy's cat experiences. Until Cleopatra, cats were lumped together on the Aggravation Scale somewhere between dryer lint and sandy spinach.

As if on cue, Cleo kneaded her claws through the soft blanket and lightly pricked the skin of Poppy's leg.

"Okay, okay. I'm awake." She pulled her leg away from the sting of Cleo's lovemaking and lost herself in ecstasy as Belle's small hand crept under her pajama top, then down her abdomen to rest warmly on her pubic mound. *Glory. Absolute glory.*

Belle turned and nuzzled her lips against Poppy's neck, then retrieved her dental bridge from a small cup beside the bed, deftly inserted it and said, smiling, "Mornin', Butterfly."

Her own wide, happy grin made it difficult to talk, but Poppy managed. "To you too, m'dear."

Belle sat up, making getting-up movements as she spoke. "So what's on the agenda for today?"

"Well, I called both Bubba and Barnes last night, hoping they could come out today and we could get Violet's drawings out of that old well, but Barnes will be in court all day and Bubba has to go to Dallas with Red for some kind of do at the Women's Shelter." Poppy swung her feet off the bed and played a quick game of get-the-rat-under-the-blanket with a pouncing, mock-ferocious Cleo.

"And Zoe and Marcie are going to be busy in town today, arranging financing to build a house on the land that Nan left Zoe." She squinted at Belle as she cleaned her glasses on the hem of her pajama top. "I guess that means Zoe is serious about Marcie being her one true love. Marcie's had a tough life, but I've never known a woman with a bigger heart. Looks like those two've just been marking time until they finally met."

Belle smiled and nodded her agreement. "I wish my daughters had turned out more like Marcie. But, it's my fault they didn't. I raised them to fit in with the world, to marry and have children and be happily married to some nice young man."

Belle's smile faded at the evident pain of her late-life discovery of the Great Patriarchal Lie. "Well, I can't dwell on that now. I did the best I could, the best I knew how." She shrugged and Poppy could almost see the troubled years slide away like an untied cloak as Belle shook herself, wet puppy-like, and brought her attention back to the present moment. "And so. Like I said, what are *we* going to do today?"

"I'm anxious to see what condition that old well is in. I think we ought to take a look at it and I want to look around the guest house a bit more. Bubba says we can go in the house now. They're through with it." She looked hopefully at Belle. "D'you think Violet would mind if we stayed down there tonight?"

"I don't think she'll mind, but I'll ask her. I

115

imagine anything you can do to get her out of this mess'll be okay with her." Belle looked back at Poppy, a worried frown creasing her forehead. "Do you think we'll be safe there, Papillon? Now that I have something to live for, I'm in no hurry to put myself in danger. And since *you're* that something . . . Well . . ."

Poppy could not have put it better herself, so she said so. "I think we'll be okay. And I feel exactly the same way about either of us being in danger. Let's just take real good care of each other, okay?" She hugged Belle fiercely and listened to the little woman's breathing become calm.

There was another reason Poppy wanted to stay at the guest house, but she wasn't yet ready to voice her suspicions. She was still puzzled at Bitsy Drake's admission of knowledge of J.C.'s whereabouts. And the nasty attitude of her protective father. She wanted to meet them both face to face and come to her own conclusions about what was going on at that secluded studio where trucks with long-haired drivers from Montana came to pick up cargo. Faraway Montana with its Canadian border.

And who had tinkered with the brakes on the jeep? Someone wanted them to stop their investigation. And dead would do it. Dead P.I.'s ask no more questions. Just like dead dykes from California have no babies or inherit no property or spend no money. Yes. A visit to Ditsy Bitsy was the next item on Poppy's list. For sure. And could it be that Poppy's feelings for Belle had tarnished her objectivity when it came to Violet's guilt or non-guilt? Surely Violet hadn't killed Morgana. But then . . .

everything pointed to her. Poppy would have to be shrewd indeed, and fair. Very fair.

* * * * *

After breakfast with Violet, Poppy and Belle and Cleo left for their overnight stay at the guest house. Lupe had packed them a picnic basket. The winds had begun to blow from the south, making the day seem almost perfect for an outdoor adventure. The winter sun shone warmly through the R.V. windows, prompting both women to remove their jackets.

Poppy used Zoe's keys to open the house, Bubba having confiscated the one under the rock. She then backed the Chinook into the oversized garage and closed the overhead pull-down door snugly past the front bumper of the vehicle.

They unloaded the R.V. and entered the house from the garage. Poppy deposited the basket on the kitchen countertop and raised an eyebrow at Belle. "Yes, I'm coming with you," Belle answered the unasked question.

They walked through the crime from probable entrance at the front door to the final blow to an imaginary Morgana's head beside the hot tub in the bathroom. Bubba had said the cause of death was drowning. The victim was first addled by the cranial injury, then slipped or was pushed under water. No fingerprints except Morgana's and Violet's in the bathroom. Some of Violet's in the rest of the house and a few of Morgana's. And most conspicuously — Violet's prints on the murder weapon.

The obvious motive for killing Morgana was the

117

inheritance. But, what if there was another reason? Was J.C. indeed around somewhere? Could he have done it from rage and frustration — or for possible gain if all *legal* inheritors were killed off? Could Bitsy have killed from the age-old motive of jealousy? She might have been jealous of Morgana having J.C.'s baby. Would bitter Collin Drake have had any reason for murder? Would Poppy and Belle be in danger if they stayed in the house? Poppy's head whirled as she and Belle migrated back to the kitchen. The sun streaming through the wide front windows beckoned them to dine outside on the deck. Once outside, Poppy shook off the dark thoughts and turned her eyes to the sky.

"My mama used to call this kind of day a weather breeder," she commented as they spread a blue and green tartan plaid cloth over a round table in the lee of the protecting chimney-wall of the house.

"A weather breeder?"

"Yeah. She always said a little norther followed by a real warm day between Thanksgiving and Christmas meant some really crazy weather was on its way." Poppy scanned the sky for signs and was rewarded by the discovery of a gray-blue line of clouds lying along the northern horizon past the smoke that drifted from the kilns behind Bitsy Drake's studio. "See yonder." She pointed at the cloudline.

"That means a cold front's on the way. When it meets up with all this warm moisture coming up from the Gulf, we're in for a big blow of some kind." Poppy frowned, remembering that they wouldn't be able to extract Violet's drawings from the well until tomorrow. And probably by then they would all freeze their collective buns off. The coming weather reminded her knee of its expected effects and a fiery twinge traveled along her shin and settled into a dull ache beneath her kneecap. She absently rubbed her knee with one hand and Cleo with the other as Belle spread their lunch.

They ate thick, turkey-on-rye sandwiches and crunchy dill pickles and sipped hot decaf coffee from Poppy's ancient Stanley thermos bottle. They sat quietly, enjoying each other's company. Poppy'd had many happy days in her life, but none — none at all like this — since Irma died.

A single crow settled on the windmill tower below them, cawing into the silence of their precious afternoon. Cleo watched the bird from her perch along the deck rail. A few fluffy white clouds gathered in the north, bumping against the growing line of dark blue along the horizon, piling up, their gray underbellies pregnant with storms and rumors of storms.

They had put away their picnic basket and tidied the table when Belle said, "Poppy, I know you can hardly wait to look down that well. Let's get your flashlight and see if we can see anything. It won't hurt just to *look*. I know we have to wait for the others for it to be official, but . . . just one little *look*?"

Poppy grinned at Belle's reading of her poorly hidden intent and promptly forgot her knee. They walked down the rocky road past clumps of brushy green cedars and tall, bare-limbed oaks trimmed with lush runners of poison ivy. Cleo's gray coat glistened as she stepped from the road to inspect the purple fox-berries that peeked around deadfalls of old wood.

119

Golden winter grass nodded seeded heads against the lightly swirling winds.

Great time of year. No chiggers, no mosquitoes, no ticks, no sweat. Just skirt the poison ivy and we'll be okeydoke.

As they neared the old homestead, Poppy noticed signs of human habitation. Wire-scarred trees, rusty wheel rims, occasional sparkles as sunlight caught broken pieces of colored glass in the ditches and small stream beds they crossed.

The old homestead had been built on the crest of a small hill. Hand-hewn blocks of sandstone from the foundation pillars lay scattered about. The timbers of the house had long since succumbed to fire and scavengers. No buildings remained standing. Only the windmill, most probably the latest addition to the place, stuck up in the air, its blades securely tied so it could not run free in the wind. Spears of dead weeds emerged from the top of a cracked, rectangular cement tank that flanked the windmill tower.

This arrangement, Poppy knew, would have served to supply both the house and livestock with water. It was a much more efficient method than the old well whose stone top was visible some yards away. Poppy hoped it was a dry well that would easily yield the roll of drawings that would make Violet Cooper's alibi more believable.

Poppy noted the wide tracks made by the tires of a heavy vehicle where it had veered off the road and across what had once been a drive of sorts in front of the house. The tall dead grass was still mashed down where Violet's big Cadillac had rolled to a stop near the windmill. Poppy wrote those observations in her little notebook, then set her shoulders and walked toward the well.

The well was artistically constructed of flat native stones laid in circular courses. Poppy imagined the mustachioed man on the horse in the sepia print from the mantle — could almost see him laying the stones, trowelling the sticky mortar, the pistol stuck into his belt, ready to defend the land he presumed to be his, by right of white male supremacy, against those from whom it was, in actuality, stolen.

The well was uncovered. Its black mouth yawned up at Poppy as she prepared to illuminate its secrets. She braced her left hand against the top and leaned forward to better see the inside.

The light did not reflect back from a watery surface as Poppy had feared it might. But from what she *could* see, she deduced the well had been used as a catchall for trash and unwanted farm machinery.

The hole was evidently shaped like a round bottle with a long slender top. The rounded-out bottom of the well was almost full of junk. A mound of it rose toward the center about twenty feet down, almost reaching the place where the walls narrowed. If the drawings were down there, they had rolled off toward the outer edge of the mound, out of sight.

Someone would have to go down there and search for the physical evidence of Violet Cooper's dreams. Poppy shuddered at the prospect and felt Belle's welcome hand on her neck. How could the touch of one small hand bring such a feeling of calm and courage?

Whoa-up right here — right now — Wondercrone!
You ain't goin' down there. End of story.

"Well . . . now . . ." Poppy mused out loud.

Ding dong bell — Poppy's in th' well, who'll get'er out?

"Yeah . . . okay . . . right. Dumb idea." She spoke aloud once more to her inner voice, then realized Belle was eyeing her quizzically.

"Sometimes the dialogue runneth over." She grinned sheepishly as Belle shook her head in a no-motion.

Belle answered, "Well, I agree that it's a dumb idea if you were entertaining even one *thought* of going down that hole!" Belle squeezed Poppy's hand and started to speak again but was distracted by a movement behind Poppy. She cupped her hands and shouted. "Cleo. Cleopatra you bad girl! Come back here!"

Poppy turned just in time to see, some hundred yards away, the white flash of Cleo's tail as the errant cat disappeared into the brush between them and the corner of Bitsy Drake's studio.

"Here, kitty — kitty — kit — kit — kit — kitty!" Belle called, with no result. Cleo did not return. "Let's give her a minute or two to come back on her own. If she doesn't, we'll have to go after her. She never misbehaves this way. I wonder what got into her?"

More calling did not have the desired result. It was as if the red land had swallowed the curious cat. Poppy couldn't decide if what she felt was truly anxiety for the cat's welfare or anguish at Belle's obvious fear and distress. Privately she thought she couldn't have contrived a better way to gain access to the reclusive artist's studio.

She did the necessary pull-up-top-strand, hold-down-bottom exercise on the barbed wire fence so Belle could climb through unscathed, and was pleased when Belle immediately executed the same maneuver so Poppy could bend and step between the dangerous wires.

Smoke curled from two large, beehive shaped brick kilns that sat apart from a large square workroom. A great mound of uniformly cut and neatly stacked firewood rose behind the kilns like a Lincoln-Log fort. A door that had been standing ajar shut with a bang just as they rounded the corner. Poppy was positive she had seen the tip of Cleo's tail in the dark portion of the doorway just before it had closed.

They looked at each other and shrugged, then nodded in unison. Poppy grinned reassuringly and knocked loudly. The door opened immediately with an outward *whoosh,* as if someone had been standing with a hand on the knob.

"I guess you want that cat," a very short woman barked at them. "Wait here." The door slammed shut.

The two startled women who stood on the stoop shared an incredulous look then waited for the door to reopen. After what seemed like much longer but was probably only a couple of minutes, Belle raised her fist and thumped loudly on the door. A muffled voice came faintly to their ears. "Hold your horses. I'll be there in a minute."

The door slowly opened and a windmilling, protesting Cleo was unceremoniously thrust toward them. Belle gathered her up quickly. Poppy stuck her foot in the door as it began to close. "Uh, wait a minute. Ms. Drake? Won't you please give us a little time. I just have a few questions."

The pressure of the door increased across Poppy's

ankle. She leaned close to it and said through the crack, "I need to get a message to J.C."

The door began to ease back until Poppy could see into the well-lit workroom. The small woman stood away from the open door. Poppy stepped into the room with Belle and a calmer Cleo close at her backside. An acrid odor of paint and musty fabric seemed to fill the inside of Poppy's head as her eyes adjusted to the different light.

Dusty white bags of clay were stacked against one wall from floor to ceiling. Eerie human figures in all stages of completion, some with faces painted — some without — sat or stood or reclined about the area.

Poppy looked closely at the tiny woman who must surely be Coleeta "Bitsy" Drake. Close-set but pretty blue eyes, pert uptilted nose and a very wide, sensuous Carly Simon mouth. Tendrils of black curly hair escaped from a scarf and trailed into the air around her head, waving about as if moved by static electricity.

"What's the message?" She spoke suddenly, with the brusqueness sometimes acquired by people who live alone and have no need to be solicitous or considerate of others. Poppy guessed that terse communication of needs or the efficient gathering of information were her only imperatives to speech.

Poppy said the first lie that came to mind. "Nancy Hightower had made changes in her will that concerned her brother. We need to contact him."

Bitsy Drake shook her head rapidly, setting in motion the aura of frizz around it. "J.C. doesn't care about any of that. He's happy now. That would only give him problems." A slight smile hovered around the corners of her mouth, but she pursed her lips together, cutting it off.

"Well," Poppy began, desperate for some kind of breakthrough. "Then please just tell him this, if you can get a message to him. Tell him I know why he took his daddy's pistol and I think he was right to do it, that I don't believe he was really a coward."

Sudden fire bloomed behind Bitsy's blue eyes and her face became instantly mobile at Poppy's last words.

Bull's-eye? Wondercrone, you perceptive old debbul.

"Oh. But he *was* a coward . . . but . . . well, he's changed now though." Bitsy Drake got hold of herself, changed direction. "He's different now." Her incendiary anger faded and her face closed. "I'll give him your message."

She turned toward the door clearly dismissing her unwelcome guests. "Go now. And get that damn cat out of here. It got hairs all over the birthday room." She gestured at a doorway in the far corner and then began to shoo them back toward the outside world.

– 13 –
All Hell Busts Loose

Poppy sat inside the wide front window of the guest house watching the clouds gather and build into a formidable wall of bluish gray, topped by the popcorn-shaped edges of numerous thunderheads. They boiled slowly up and up into the ethereal reaches of the evening atmosphere as the whole mass of unstable air moved inexorably toward Red Rook Ranch.

"Gonna be one helluva storm here about midnight

I figure," Poppy informed Belle, who'd come to stand behind her chair. The lights in Bitsy Drake's studio across the little valley blinked out at the same moment the lights came on in the separate A-frame house that Bitsy lived in. Poppy rose from her chair and paced for a minute. Cleopatra, her self-appointed shadow, paced behind her, turning when she did, executing quick but efficient ankle-veronicas each time Poppy stood still.

Belle asked, "What's on your mind, dear? What's going on under those beautiful white curls?"

Poppy turned away from the window. "Well. Ummm." She tried to think of an easy way to tell Belle what she wanted to do. Finding nothing, she plunged ahead. "I keep going over what happened at Bitsy's studio this afternoon. That loony little woman is hiding something. I'd bet my life on it."

Belle looked meaningfully toward the bathroom where Morgana had recently lost a similar wager, and shivered. "I certainly hope it doesn't come down to that."

Poppy's hand crept into the pocket of her sleeveless vest to rest on the comfortingly solid butt of her pistol. She ran her thumbnail down the checkered ridges of the handle as she continued. "And what the hell do you s'pose a birthday room is? Did you see the deranged glint in her eyes when she talked about that? I've got a hunch there's something right over there in that workroom of hers that will help put this puzzle together!"

"And so you want to go over there and poke around? Is that what you're trying to tell me?" Belle asked, a worried frown creasing her forehead.

"Well . . . yes. The lock on that door is just a

simple tab type. I think I can get it open pretty quick." *Ah yes, Wondercrone, the great P.I., picks the lock with her handy-dandy, buck-ninety-eight Tickalock Pickalock.*

Belle answered quickly, but her voice held a tiny quaver. "Okay, but only if I can go with you. I don't want to stay here alone, Poppy. I'm frightened." Cleo meowed her agreement with Belle's confession.

Joplin was right, wasn't she, Dillworth? Freedom's just another name for nothin' left to lose! Now that we got a lot to live for, the risking takes real courage, doesn't it, W.C.?

"I believe I'm a bit frightened too, Belle. It'd be real dumb not to be, considering everything that's happened. But something in me has to solve this puzzle. Some ole grizzly bear has finally waked up mean and hungry somewhere about here!" She jabbed a finger toward her solar plexus for emphasis, feeling the rolling sum total of all those inactive years behind the despised typewriter. Not allowed to contribute, not permitted to help when she knew she could do the job — and do it better, by Goddess!

"I know, dear," Belle answered softly, and pressed her small warm body close to Poppy. "I have my own bears to feed, you know."

Poppy knew.

Her eyes filled with tears at the sudden rush of love and physical feeling that gathered inside her. A wave that washed over the grizzly in her gut, calming it for a moment, then moved outward through trunk and arms and legs and settled in her vagina and groin with a powerful, beautiful, hurtful surge. She guided Belle toward a nearby sofa. To sit down before her weakened knees betrayed her.

They hugged and kissed and stroked Cleo for a few moments, sitting before the window, watching the darkness grow full and inky. Lightning flashes illuminated the inner reaches of the now much nearer clouds, blooming yellow-white and orange against the purple and black sky. The wind had swung around now and blew steadily from the north, carrying chill messages from Canada on its breath. Poppy knew it was the kind of chill that could bring frozen precipitation of almost any kind. Not a night to tarry long out of doors.

"Let's do it, Watson." Poppy said, resolve strong in her voice.

"Okay. I'm ready, lead on," Belle answered in tones to match, clearly primed for action.

* * * * *

They locked the nervous cat in the R.V. in the garage. It was the safest, most comfortable place Poppy could think of for Cleo to stay while they searched for secrets in the night. Both women pulled on jackets, hats and gloves — checked flashlights, keys, pocket knives, camera and pistol — and left the house.

They kept to the road so they wouldn't need to use the flashlight. Constant lightning chased itself inside the clouds, covering one whole half of the big inverted bowl of Texas sky that seemed to cup the earth, concentrating the glowing, green-tinged electrical display into an eons-traveled weather path across southern Oklahoma and northern Texas. The river, visible at times in the distance beyond the leafless trees, reflected the eerie light in a moving, broken glow like cooling lava.

The quiet — pregnant with the absence of thunder — surrounded Poppy and Belle. Soon the storms would move near enough for the constant rolling booms to reach them, but now they heard only the cold wind rustling through vegetation and their own careful footsteps.

They left the road just past the homestead and the creaking windmill, and Poppy had to turn on her flashlight. She'd taped brown paper around the red end of it to block its signalling effect and it glowed dimly like a luminaria as she moved through the fence and held the spiky wires apart for Belle.

Poppy searched the sky for the moon. She usually knew its phases. Her friend Lu Blassingame from Houston had given her a goddess-moon calendar and she wore a moon-phase watch. But the expected three-quarter gibbous moon had not risen yet, or, if it had, was hidden behind the growing mound of clouds.

Poppy's senses were cranked up to their most alert. She jerked in surprise as Belle grasped her around the waist from behind, a split-second after a nearby band of startled coyotes yipped a warning into the night.

She turned and hugged Belle close, feeling the pounding of their two frightened hearts merge into a kind of low sonorous hum. As if in echo, the first hollow *bump-bump* of thunder made itself audible.

"Whew . . ." Poppy whispered. "Guess we'd

better get on with this caper before we get caught by the weather."

Belle giggled softly against Poppy's collarbone. "Yeah, or before the coyotes give us a collective heart attack."

"Storm must've stirred 'em up."

They moved apart and resumed their journey. The square black mass of Bitsy's workroom loomed suddenly before them. Poppy gave Belle the flashlight to hold as she deftly manipulated a ring of metal picks. She chose a specific size and shape and inserted it into the keyhole. All those years of teasing she'd endured while she practiced with the picks during lunch breaks had finally paid off. She wanted to throw her knitted watch cap into the air and hoot her victory loudly into the night, but instead just grinned so wide her teeth grew cold as the lock clicked under her gloved hand and the door opened slowly outward.

Belle was almost glued to Poppy's backside as they stepped cautiously inside. The figures that in daylight had looked merely strange now appeared menacing. A live human could easily hide by simply remaining still among all the other similar shapes. Poppy led Belle through them on her way toward the doorway in the corner that Bitsy had pointed to during her animated conversation earlier that day.

The birthday room? Poppy had no doubt that it was significant to the solution of one or more puzzles. She relished the rush of chills that gathered under her shoulder blades and zoomed up her spine to raise the hair at the nape of her neck. The *feeling*. God how she loved it! The exciting feeling of anxious anticipation she always experienced when she was on the verge of an important discovery.

Her hand trembled a little as she reached the door, turned the knob and pulled. To her surprise the door opened easily outward revealing darkness almost fuzzy in its intensity. She shone the light straight in front of her, illuminating a bizarre tableau.

A table stood in the center of the small windowless room. On it sat a birthday cake with many candles. Not a real cake, Poppy decided, but something more permanent, probably from the kilns outside.

Juvenile highchairs flanked the table on one side, each one occupied by the same childish figure. No. Not the same. Each one seemed a little different from its neighbor. The same male child, but older maybe? Yes. That must be it. Poppy threw light on each figure in turn until she had seen the somehow familiar little boy grow to long-haired, hippy-like porcelain manhood. A young man who, except for close-set eyes and too-wide mouth, looked mighty like J.C. Junior had in his school yearbook senior class picture. Like J.C. Junior had looked the last time anyone had seen him on Red Rook Ranch.

"Jesusmaryandjoseph!" Poppy said aloud as realization dawned on her. In her excitement, the goddess of recently embraced feminism took a back seat to the gods of her childhood.

Belle spoke in hushed wonderment. "You know who that boy has to be, don't you, Poppy?"

"Yeah . . . has to be what a child of J.C. Hightower and Coleeta Drake would look like. Black hair, close together blue eyes, and that wide mouth."

Poppy gave the light to Belle, pointed her camera

132

at different sections of the strange scene and snapped. The flashes sent little red dots pinballing against the inside of her eyelids.

The icy downdraft from the rapidly advancing line of thunderstorms pressed suddenly across the little valley. It slammed shut the workroom outer door with a crash that caused Poppy's heart to flutter. She thrust the camera into her pocket and groped toward Belle for the flashlight.

Belle's fingers were like steel cables as Poppy tried to pry loose the small Eveready from her grasp.

"It's okay, honey," Poppy whispered. "It was just the storm. Let's get out of here."

Belle's fingers slowly loosened and Poppy slipped the flashlight away from her. They made their way back to the main room and once again weaved their way between the eerie figures. Belle was as close to Poppy as separate skins and individual clothing would allow. They moved to the door stepping in unison like two partners in a sack race.

The wind howled and continuous lightning flashes brightened the landscape for seconds at a time until it looked more like day than night, except that the brilliance of the white light leached all color from the scene outside the windows. It flickered white and gray and black like an old silent film.

Okay, Dillworth. There ain't no guy in the wings going to pound on a piano as a cue for you to open that door!

Poppy quickly opened it, set the lock button, grabbed Belle's hand and they bent their heads into the wind. The door knob slipped from Poppy's grasp and the door slammed shut.

The booming roar of thunder rattled the window

panes behind them. Poppy felt the sound vibrating in her lungs. "Jee-zus!" she exploded as freezing rain drove straight at them, flying almost level to the ground. They were pelted with dust, dirt and sand driven by the intense wind.

"Follow me," Poppy yelled in Belle's direction, the shouted words barely audible, taken from her mouth and flung into the maelstrom.

Poppy jammed the unnecessary flashlight into her pocket and she and Belle broke into a modified trot, prodded by the wind at their backs. They repeated their return passage through the barbed wire fence. The windmill blades had broken free and whizzed and pinged in a wild dance of freedom.

Poppy cast a glance at Bitsy Drake's cottage to see if her lights were still on. Her thudding heart leaped as she realized she saw no lights at all. None at Bitsy's and none at the guest house. The storm was already taking its toll on the rural electrification system.

Belle bounded up the few steps and onto the guest house deck in front of Poppy with the key in her fingers leading the way. She opened the door swiftly and closed it after Poppy stepped into the darkened room.

* * * * *

Although Poppy thought it unlikely anyone would venture out into the storm, she did think they ought to satisfy themselves there were no intruders either under beds or in closets. A cautious, room-to-room search accomplished nothing except the elevation of blood pressure and fearful teeth grinding. It played on Poppy's mind a bit that she had braved the storm, and so might have others.

They finally sat huddled together on a loveseat in front of a dark, cold fireplace for which there was no wood except for stacks outside which could stay there until the devil ice skated, they both agreed.

"Ohmygod — *Cleo!*" Belle leaped up, startling Poppy. "She must be frightened to death. She *hates* thunder!"

So — Herself is a fraidy-cat, is she? The great one has paws of clay. Poppy suppressed a giggle at her inner cantankerousness and said aloud, "Well, since it's cold and dark in here, why don't we go join her in the R.V.? I've got some cozy sleeping bags out there and we can have lights from the battery for a while." She looked at Belle's face for clues as to how she felt about this suggestion, but the lightning had abated and she could only see a pale, face-shaped glow in front of her.

But she got her answer as Belle sat down abruptly and clasped her arms round Poppy in a miniature bearhug. "Oh, could we? Please? Right now?"

They raided the refrigerator by flashlight, and carried the remains of their picnic to their enforced campout in the garage.

Cleo yowled pitifully from her confines in the Chinook. Poppy opened the front door cautiously but she and Belle were no match for the frightened cat. She dashed past them and raced around the garage.

"She can't get out can she?" Belle asked.

"Nope . . . but we need to put her litter box out

here for a while," Poppy answered, as she sniffed the air in the cab. "I don't think she's had any accidents in here, but you can't ever tell."

"Oh. Well, okay . . . but Cleo's much too well-behaved for *that*."

Poppy kept silent, remembering one of her few feline experiences. Irma had tomcat-sat for a friend and the animal had sprayed everything in the house that belonged to Poppy. Not Irma's, just Poppy's. Of course, she supposed female cats might behave differently, but the incident had made a lasting impression. She'd had to give all her clothes to the Goodwill people. Ellie, her beloved springer spaniel, had pouted in the corner, wouldn't even come near her — no matter how many times she washed her jeans. Her chest tightened and a lump worked in her throat at the memory of Ellie. What a dog. Someday she must get another dog. She missed having one.

She was barely conscious of Belle retrieving Cleo from the wilds of the garage and bringing her inside the R.V. She worked at folding out the bed while her mind filled with memories of the one and only time Irma had gotten to sleep in the R.V. The plans they'd made for Poppy's retirement. The months of shopping and finally settling on the Toyota Chinook.

Then that shattering day when Irma had told Poppy the awful truth about the cancer and how long she might expect to live. In fact, Irma had died mercifully sooner than the doctor's prognosis.

Belle, who'd been fixing them a snack, sat beside Poppy and took her hand. "What's wrong? You look so sad."

Poppy faced her, swallowed back the lump that threatened emergence of tears. "I was thinking of

Irma, and how we planned for my retirement. How many wonderful places we planned to go in this thing." She stood and looked out the R.V. window past the panes of the garage window, watching the flashes of the receding storm.

She felt Belle standing close behind her. "Poppy. Look at me."

Poppy turned.

"I know I can never take Irma's place. But I can be a *new* presence in your life if you'll let me. I've never experienced a feeling or emotion equal to what I'm feeling for you this minute. I love you, Papillon." She nodded in the direction of Cleo, who now happily reclined on the bed between the pillows. "Have cat, will travel. How about it? Interested?"

Poppy felt the mama grizzly roll over inside her, playing with cubs, deliriously scooping honey and grubs from logs, running full tilt toward a salmon-choked falls — a yell formed down in her abdomen, rose to her lungs and rushed out her mouth as she tilted her head back and *yaahooed* unbridled happiness at the ceiling of the camper.

Cleo sprang out of their way as Poppy tumbled Belle onto the bed in a laughing, snuggling celebration.

Belle asked breathlessly, "Does this mean you're interested?"

The leprechaun appeared again in Poppy's heart, dancing a now familiar jig. She calmed herself a bit and managed to answer somewhat levelly. "Yes. *Yes* Belle. I'm interested. I love you, too." Oh, how good to say it. How good to *feel* it. She held Belle away from her for a moment. Her braided hair had come loose and trailed down her shoulders and her brown eyes flashed up at Poppy, sending an invitation for a much more physical type of celebration.

They shared their passion, warm under the quilted covers of the sleeping bag. Poppy exulted in Belle's unbridled enthusiasm to learn how Poppy needed to be touched. Her hot and breathless insistence on sliding beneath the covers to explore with her lips and tongue. Belle's girlish pride when she brought a surprised Poppy to orgasm a second time. And Poppy made love to Belle. With patience and skill and loving playfulness she showered Belle's small body with every caress, every attention she could stay calm enough to recall. Again and again Belle arched toward Poppy's hands, her mouth, the mound of her vulva as they writhed together like two dolphins in an underwater dance of love.

Afterward, as they sat holding hands over the tiny table, their mouths full of food, their eyes declaring outrageous thoughts, Belle swallowed and said, "You know, Papillon, I believe I've been a lesbian all my life. Is it possible to be one in all ways except this final, physical expression of woman love?"

"Well . . . sure. Sure it is. But I'm glad I was here for you to land on when you took that final leap."

Belle smiled back at her from dark, happy eyes. "Me too," she answered simply.

Poppy nodded, rose and shined the flashlight so it illuminated the air outside the garage window. "I thought so, look at that!" She pointed at the white pellets moving through the beam of light like meteors. "Sleet . . . sonuvagun! Wonder if the lights ever came back on? I'll go in and check."

She left Belle and Cleo in the safety of the R.V. and returned to the house. She flicked a switch. *Nope, no lights.* She snapped a few more switches to make sure. Intending to call Zoe and let them know she and Belle were okay, she picked up the phone. Dead silence. No hollow clicks or buzzing. Just nothing. Must be a tree down somewhere, she thought.

She hoped.

The hair on her neck rose as her thoughts took a fearful turn. *Nahh.* It was just the storm. She moseyed back to the garage, playing an elaborately casual game of don't-hurry-cause-if-the-monster-knows-you're-scared-it'll-getchooo-ooo.

Soon she was snuggled spoon fashion against Belle and drifted into sleep with a purring Cleo stretched across the pillow above their heads like a vibrating, fur-covered heating pad.

* * * * *

Poppy awoke a few hours later, she didn't know what time, it was still dark. A popping, roaring noise filled her ears. Hail? Not likely. The blustery front had passed through. The conditions were now too cold for hail. What, then? Sleet? Poppy opened her eyes wider and could barely make out the window. A rosy glow began to define the shape of the rectangle while she watched. Must be morning.

Sunrise?

No! Too fast.

She struggled out of the sleeping bag, jammed her glasses on her nose and leaped to her feet. A string of sparks spewed past the window in long swirls, like fireworks on the wind.

Fire! The goddamn house is on fire! Think Papillon! What — what — what're we gonna —

"Belle! Get up! Get in the front seat and put your head down low on your knees . . . Up! Do it!"

Poppy sprang to the driver's seat and ground the key in the ignition. "C'mon Diehard, don't let me down!" Oh God, had she burned the lights too long? But Belle had been so lovely, Belle's brown eyes. "C'mon, sonuvabitch! *Start!*"

The tough battery delivered the power and the engine roared to life. Poppy silently thanked God and Sears and Roebuck.

Poppy shouted at Belle who was now beside her in the other captain's chair, "Hang on, honey. We're bustin' out of here!" She eased into reverse, backed slowly until she felt a light bump, getting all the running room she could for their forward thrust through the closed garage door.

In the side mirrors she saw a shower of sparks fall from the garage ceiling and land smoking on the steps that led from the garage into the house. The garage suddenly filled with dense smoke. The headlights were like two white shafts attached to the front grill.

Time to go!

Now!

She dropped the transmission into low, eased down on the accelerator, braking with the other foot.

Off the brake!

GO!

The tires whizzed, squealing against the cement

floor, then grabbed and they shot forward, a Toyota juggernaut aimed at freedom.

Poppy held the steering wheel in an iron grip when the front bumper hung on a steel rod as they crashed through the door pulling the little R.V. around in a sickening sideways skid. She jammed her foot hard on the gas pedal, pulled the wheel in the opposite direction and they popped free, bouncing down the drive far too fast to stop at the sleet-covered road.

Poppy pulled around sharply, slowed the careening Chinook and managed to pull parallel to the road into first one ditch, then across to the other, then to the middle of the road. Finally the vehicle took a sideways skid and stopped, the one working headlight pointed back up toward the house.

Poppy and Belle watched in horror as the main roof exploded in a volcano of blowing sparks and a great spiraling column of flame. Then the garage roof dipped and fell in on the place where they had been parked until thirty seconds ago.

A muffled yowling from behind them spurred Belle from her seat. Poppy turned to see a lumpy sleeping bag creeping along the floor toward them. Belle peeled it back to reveal a very shaky, wild-eyed Cleo.

"Poor baby. Come to Mama." Belle firmly held the frightened cat and crooned to her. Then she looked at Poppy with her eyes so big the whites showed all the way around her pupils.

"It wasn't an accident, was it Poppy?"

"I don't know," Poppy lied. "Coulda been. Storm and all." She didn't tell Belle what she had just seen. That the lights were on over at Bitsy's studio. Or

141

that a movement through the woods looked mighty like someone backing out of the light thrown by the burning house.

"What we gotta do now is get to the ranch before we lose all the coolant out of this baby. 'Pears we've sprung a leak." She pointed at the crumpled hood, where vents of steam had begun to issue from the general area of the radiator. She glanced at the heat indicator and saw it had begun to move upward.

Poppy carefully righted the R.V. on the icy road and they started for the ranch. The landscape had changed overnight to winter white. Sparkling drifts of sleet fingered down onto the road from the fence rows.

The sky above the eastern horizon began to glow with suffused light, but there was no color. The lowering clouds were thick and gray, packed woolly-ridged tight, covering the whole sky from horizon to horizon. And a fierce north wind blew relentlessly at them, carrying tiny flakes of the season's first snow.

"We're gonna make it, honey." Poppy spoke reassuringly, but her stomach was knotted with tension. She realized she was cold and her bare feet on the floorboard were icy. As if reading her thoughts, Belle held her jacket around her so she could insert one arm at a time.

The guardlight by the vehicle barn twinkled at them through the predawn gloom. *Just one more hill, babe, just one more itty-bitty hill.* Poppy silently coaxed the little Toyota engine. The yellow needle on the heat indicator had been above the red disaster level for at least the last mile. They chugged and slipped to the crest of the last rise where Poppy gratefully cut the engine and they coasted toward Zoe's cabin.

She pressed the heel of her hand against the horn button, more in celebration than as a means of attracting attention from the cabin's sleeping occupants. The long stuttering nasal *beeeep* announced their progress over the last hundred yards.

She set the brake as they drew even with the carport where the jeep sat out of the weather. Poppy felt her arms begin to tremble and tears roll down her cheeks as Belle held her tightly. So close. They'd come *so close* to losing everything. To death. To being gone.

She smiled through her tears as Zoe burst out the front door clad only in boots and a short trader-blanket robe. Whirling like a blonde, long-legged Jimminy Cricket, trying to cover her naked bottom exposed by the wind.

– 14 –
Marcie's Scoop

A hectic half hour later, after Violet had been informed of the night's events, Poppy and Belle sat across the table from Zoe and Marcie in Zoe's bright little kitchen. Their story of the storm, the fire, their Dukes-of-Hazard escape from the garage and the harrowing trip back to the ranch met with appropriate open-mouthed awe.

"You mean the fire had been burning long enough

for the roof to fall in just after you crashed out?" Marcie asked.

"Yeppers. Musta been set to burn the bedrooms first. The garage was the last place to go," Poppy answered, trying to clean her glasses with one hand and rub her tired eyes with the other.

Zoe asked, incredulously, "You really think someone tried to *kill* y'all?"

Poppy glanced at Belle briefly before she answered. "Yeah . . . I do. I didn't say anything to Belle about something I saw as we left." She felt Belle stiffen beside her. "Looked like someone stepping into the woods, away from the light and heat of the fire. Couldn't make out who — not even if it was a man or woman. Just caught an impression of a human figure backing away, arm thrown up over their face. Like the sudden burst of heat got to 'em."

Zoe was the first one to find her voice. "Well, Bubba's 'sposed to come out today and get Violet's drawings out of the old well. I guess now he can come earlier and take a look at what used to be the guest house." Zoe ran her long fingers through her sleep-mussed hair as she spoke, her other arm snuggled in the soft curve of Marcie's waist.

Poppy sensed a strong bond between the two women and it warmed her heart. *Yep, Dillworth — looks like some happy-ever-after goin' on here.* She grinned to herself as she remembered how comical Zoe had been, dancing on the ice-covered front stoop in her birthday suit.

Birthday.

"Hey," Poppy said, "We forgot to tell you about our nighttime visit to Bitsy's studio." Attentive faces

145

turned toward her as she, with Belle's help, told Marcie and Zoe about the trip through the woods and their discovery of the bizarre birthday room.

Zoe looked suddenly thoughtful. "D'you 'spose J.C.'s been coming back all these years to visit that crazy little woman? I been thinking about all those trucks coming in and out. Woulda been easy, you know. Way out there in the boonies like that." She warmed to her theory supporting the possible guilt of her favorite suspect. "He had motive *and* opportunity, Poppy."

Marcie said, "I've got some juicy stuff to tell y'all that might help make some sense of Bitsy's birthday room." Barely able to suppress her excitement, she jiggled on the edge of her chair.

Zoe turned to her, encouraging. "You holdin' back on me, babe?" She poked Marcie playfully in the general area of her ribs. "C'mon. Out with it."

"Well." Marcie sucked in a big lungful of air, preparatory to speaking. Her large breasts swelled out like rapidly rising dough.

Fourty-four double-D, or I've lost my eye completely, Poppy registered mentally.

"Well, yesterday when we were in town about the house business, while Zoe was busy at the courthouse, I decided to do a little investigating on my own." Her chest expanded again in obvious pride at her accomplishment. Poppy noticed Zoe squirm on her chair, her blue eyes doing little *nummy-nummies* at the place where Marcie's robe gaped to reveal the enticing crevice where her creamy breasts vie with each other for space.

Poppy was suddenly aware of Belle's laughing eyes on *her*. She felt the heat rise up her neck to her ears as she realized she'd been caught bosom-watching. Even Cleo in Belle's lap seemed to be watching the rise and fall of Marcie's breasts.

Marcie continued her story, unaware of the unanimous appreciation of her anatomy. "See, I figured in a small town like this, there must be somebody still around here that went to school with Coleeta Drake. "And the best place to ask questions was at the local beauty shop."

Zoe exclaimed, "I *wondered* how you got your hair to stay so pretty yesterday!"

Marcie's cheeks glowed as she went on. "Bea Brown at the Bea Dolled Salon was a cheerleader when Bitsy was drum majorette their last year in high school. She says that when J.C. Junior left that spring after graduation, everybody knew Bitsy was pregnant, and figured it had to be his kid. That those two were, she said, 'pretty much a *heavy* duo — strange y'know? Never much ever *talked* to anyone except each other. If ya know what I mean.' And I said yeah, I know! Actually after Bea got started, I just listened and said yeah a lot."

"What happened to the kid?" Zoe asked.

"I'm gettin' to that." Marcie pursed her lips at the interruption. "Bea says it was common gossip that Bitsy went off to a home for unwed mothers over at Fort Worth. But she came back without a baby, and everyone figured she gave it up for adoption. But she'd gotten an art scholarship and right away she left for someplace up east and didn't come back until two years later."

Marcie stopped for a sip of coffee, then continued. "Well, Bea says when Bitsy came back, Collin Drake, her daddy, built her that studio and A-frame down by the river. Bea said she and another girl drove out to see her one day, 'just to be *supportive,* if ya know what I mean,' and that Bitsy rushed them off the place and 'let them know she didn't *want* no support!' and I said yeah, I know what you mean.'' Marcie's eyes twinkled with excitement.

"But, what —" Poppy began, but was cut off by a wave of Marcie's hand.

"I'm not *through* yet . . . I called T.J. in Dallas and asked her to check out Bea's story and she's 'sposed to call me just as soon as she's got something.'' Marcie sat back, plainly pleased at the impact of her news on the other women.

"It may be a while before she calls, though," Poppy mused. "They guard those records like Fort Knox.''

She'd no more than closed her mouth when the ringing of the phone startled them all. Zoe leaped for it, tipping her chair over in her haste. Cleo lunged in agile haste for safer ground beneath Poppy's chair.

"'Lo . . . yeah . . . she's right here.'' Zoe glanced proudly at Marcie. "Okay. Yeah, we will, T.J. Thanks for the invite. Here's my little cupcake now.'' She handed the instrument to Marcie, who now stood at her side.

"Hi, T.J. Whatcha got? . . . *Really!* Wow! That was quick. A baby boy. Stillborn. Uh-huh, but how'd you find out so fast?'' She listened, as T.J. answered. "Well . . . my word! You did good, Charlie Brown, we appreciate it. You wanna talk to Poppy? No? Okay. I'll tell her. Yeah, I'm looking forward to meeting you too . . . a New Year's party? You bet. I can't wait. Bye.''

She hung up and turned to Poppy. "She says the

records on that case were never closed. That Coleeta Drake had intended to keep her baby but it was stillborn." She raised an eyebrow at Poppy. "Don't you think the room you and Belle discovered makes more sense now? It musta been some kind of crazy shrine to the rat who ran out on her and to her baby that died."

Too bad she's gonna retire to the ranch before she ever gets to be a full-fledged P.I., Dillworth. The girl has a real head for it.

"Good work, Marcie," Poppy praised her partner, then let her mind ramble back over the last twenty-four hours. Closer — by Goddess — she was getting closer to unraveling this mess.

Yeah. Closer. But not there yet. Too many questions. So Coleeta Drake was a loony recluse. They had known that all along. The new information made her craziness easier to understand, that's all.

But was the little woman crazy enough to try to burn them up in the guest house? Had she seen them snooping around her studio? Had she killed Morgana out of some irrational jealousy stemming from Nan's wish that Morgana bear J.C. Junior's baby? A baby that should have been Bitsy's? Instead of the porcelain baby in the birthday room?

Somehow Poppy couldn't quite believe it was Bitsy she'd seen scoot into the woods as they left the burning house. The feeling that it was a man stuck with her. J.C. maybe? And where was that damned elusive pimpernel of a brother anyway? She yearned to see the fellow face to face. How had the years changed him? What did he look like? *Could be fat and bald by now, W.C. Mighta had a sex-change operation. Josephina Calvina, maybe?*

A sudden mental image of a crow filled Poppy's mind. A crow lifting into the air from its perch on a fence post. A crow with something to say about seeing what one looked at? She made a note to review that video one more time. There was something there, she just knew there was. The crow cawed in her mental ear. A hollow, down in the culvert, Stephen King kind of sound. A sudden flash of gooseflesh raised the hair on her arms.

Way to go W.C. — spook yourself, why doncha?

– 15 –
Delbert's Discovery

Later that same day, in the early afternoon, Red Swindell called to offer her services and Delbert's, along with the four-wheel-drive Suburban, in collecting Violet for the trip to the well. And to say she was really looking forward to the chance to speak to Ms. Cooper on behalf of the children at the Women's Shelter.

And as the Swindells passed by Zoe's cabin on their way to investigate the nature of the fire at the guest house and give Violet a chance to view the damage, Poppy wished she could be a mouse in Violet's pocket. She wanted to listen in on Bubba's hyphenated, feminist-person wife who sat backwards in her seat talking and gesticulating at a captured Violet Cooper.

The sparkling clean sides of the black Suburban were barely splattered with strings of red mud. Zoe told Poppy that the vehicle was Bubba's personal transportation. That he actually owned it. The county had turned down his request for one so he had bought it himself and installed all the electronic gear into it. He was sort of Rojo county's version of Bruce Wayne.

A bubbamobile?

Poppy had laughed with the others but voiced admiration for the little guy's dedication. In her estimation, Texas could use a few more bubbas like this one.

Poppy, Belle, Marcie and Zoe boarded Zoe's jeep for the trip out to the old well at the homestead. Cleo watched reproachfully from Zoe's cabin window, suffering the ignominy of confinement to a "safe place for a nosy cat on a muddy day."

The sky had cleared about midmorning, although the air remained crisply cold. Bright sunshine pressed relentlessly on the patchy covering of snow and sleet, which began to melt and stain with orange as mud formed beneath it.

Belle gripped Poppy's arm as the charred skeleton of the cedar-and-stone guest house appeared against the hard blue sky of the near horizon. Tendrils of smoke still curled from it into the almost windless day. It was hard to imagine the ferocity of last night's storm in the calm, gentle atmosphere of the present afternoon.

Poppy placed her ungloved hand over Belle's and squeezed reassuringly. She silently agreed — life was too good to lose. They had come very close indeed to being the source of just so much greasy smoke — lost on the wind, a couple of crispy old rinds in a crumpled tin can.

Bubba's Suburban was parked on on the road below the snow-covered cactus gardens. His wife, dressed in a colorful, doubtless politically-correct poncho and magenta scarf, stood on the road, still talking to Violet who sat in the vehicle listening with uncharacteristically silent, avid interest. They both turned and waved as the jeep came nearer, but Deputy Delbert was nowhere to be seen.

As Zoe carefully pulled the jeep up behind the larger vehicle, Bubba emerged from the woods at the side of the house, wiping his hands and carrying a wad of clear plastic bags. A small but expansive-looking Pentax camera, attached to a broad strap, bumped his chest as he made his way hurriedly toward them. An assortment of black leather cases affixed to his wide belt moved when he walked, clattering and squeaking against the holster of his shiny .357 magnum.

His brown regulation Stetson was jammed incongruously over a red wool scarf that covered his ears and was fastened under his chin with the largest safety pin Poppy had ever seen. *A man with a mission. A man who doesn't give a big rat's behind what anybody thinks of him.* Mama Grizzly was proud of the boy. Yessir, he did his species proud, he did.

Bubba — seemingly unaware of anything except

his own mission to gather evidence, solve the murders, garner a little respect from Beverly, spit in Daddy Bert's eye and just maybe, along the way, become an expectant father — Bubba just kept on doing what he did best.

"You ladi — *women* ready to get the job done at the well?" He focused on Poppy, who'd rolled down her window, as he nervously cleaned mud from his boot heel with the screwdriver blade of a thick, red-handled Swiss army knife.

Poppy answered for the group as Zoe and Marcie were still ogling the smoking remains of what had almost been Poppy and Belle's tomb. "Yep, let's get it done. It's mighty cold for chit-chat."

Zoe drove the jeep around in front to lead the way. They waited while Bubba meticulously stored his plastic bags of evidence in a many-drawered cabinet in the back of the big Chevy wagon.

The hair at the nape of Poppy's neck began to lift and quiver, a little bit like the rolling, under-skin flex of a horse ridding itself of biting pests. Her excitement level was high as the group finally started for the well. She couldn't be exactly sure it all had to do with rescuing Violet's drawings from their resting place, thereby strengthening the argument for Violet's innocence.

Her agitation might, she knew, have something to do with the fact of Belle's hand sliding absently up and back along her inner thigh under cover of her pea jacket, resting warmly on occasion upon her crotch, cupping, patting, loving her in a free and simple way she'd never known. Not even with Irma had she experienced such physicality. Belle approached her lately-chosen lesbianism with a gusto that kept

154

Poppy in a state of more or less constant awareness of her own body.

And she loved it. Besides, the release of all those endorphins soothed her arthritic aches and pains. Funny — she couldn't recall even one doctor prescribing sexual excitement as a balm for aging joints.

Her attention zoomed back to the present moment as Zoe tried to brake coming over the next to last little rise before the homestead, and the jeep skidded first one way then the other across a sheet of ice still glistening hard in the shade of nearby brushy cedars.

"Whooaa girl!" Zoe whooped, as the jeep straightened itself and they began a more careful ascent of the final hill. They parked in front of the homestead, leaving plenty of room for Bubba to maneuver the Suburban close to the well, which he did easily with evident skill and judgement.

Poppy noticed there was no smoke coming from the kilns at Bitsy's today. The little valley on both sides of them seemed quiet and watching.

Waiting.

Almost like the land had been stunned into a wary silence by the fierce storm of less than twenty-four hours ago.

The women formed themselves into a loose semi-circle and watched as Bubba unloaded a ladder constructed of bright yellow nylon rope and narrow aluminum stepboards. He looked down the well once with his flashlight, then attached one end of the ladder to the Chevy bumper and dropped the rest of it into the well.

"Zoe, could you give me a hand?" He looked over at Zoe who, Poppy noted with amusement, seemed pleased at the opportunity to show off for Marcie — that same Marcie who'd been recently promoted to "cupcake" status in Zoe's world. The Marcie who would've bridled at being called cupcake a few days ago, B.Z. — Before Zoe. Poppy felt a little prickle of warning cross behind her eyes. Oh well, Zoe would just have to take care of herself. And Marcie was probably very capable of setting Zoe straight if she didn't like being thought of as junk food. *Or Sugarpie or Ladybug, Wondercrone?*

"Let's test this thing," Bubba said and placed Zoe on one side of the ladder while he took the other. They faced the bumper and leaned back hard, pulling against the knot.

The constant rattling hum of Red Swindell's chatter ceased abruptly as Violet held up a restraining hand and placed a lacquered fingernail to Red's lips.

"All right, Beverly. I'm convinced. Now let's watch your marvelous, brave husband risk his life to rescue my dead dreams from that dangerous hole!" Violet said pointedly, not skimping on the acting skills needed to convey the idea that Beverly was extremely remiss, probably even un-American, in her cavalier attitude toward her husband's derring-do.

Red looked incredulously at Violet, then around at the other women, and finally at Bubba, who stood checking over the equipment he would need for his spelunking. She seemed, Poppy thought, to suddenly see her husband as someone respected and liked by others. Maybe even as one whose *issues* might be as deserving of attention as her own.

The attention of other women?

Strong, amazon, *lesbian* women even.

Beverly jammed her hands in her jeans pockets and blushed. Her normally white skin glowed increasingly crimson until her brushy eyebrows stood out like two orange caterpillars above her eyes.

Well, how 'bout that, W.C.? The girl's got the grace to blush, at least!

"Okay. I think I'm ready." Bubba lifted himself over the stone lip and tested his weight against the ladder. "Miz Dillworth, could you stand over there and lower down anything else I might need?" He indicated a coil of rope he'd placed on the ground.

Poppy saw that she was headed off at the pass by Beverly Stand-by-her-man Swindell. "I'll do it, Delbert . . . honey," she said, as she positioned her body beside the rope.

Bubba didn't fumble the ball at the welcome but unexpected endearment, Poppy thought — but she didn't miss his wide grin as he climbed down out of sight.

Hollow clunks and muffled exclamations issued from the hole as Bubba evidently met up with the pile of trash below. Then a silence, sudden and deep, enveloped them. As it lengthened into a minute or more, Poppy's cardiac leprechaun prepared to jig.

Then Bubba's voice, a little strained, croaked up at them. "Hey up there. I found 'em. I'm coming up!" The yellow ropes of the ladder creaked against the ancient masonry and Bubba suddenly appeared, handing Red a roll of dirty white papers now safely stuffed into a long plastic bag.

Bubba then clambered unceremoniously out of the well, pulled the ladder up and also handed it to Red. "Miz Dillworth, can I see you over here privately for a minute." He nodded toward the front of the Chevy

157

and walked in that direction, leaving a surprised Poppy to follow suit.

Bubba swiped at perspiration on his upper lip, leaned close to Poppy and whispered, "There's something else down there, ma'am. Something that used to be a human being . . . a long time ago." He ran a finger under his collar, loosening the *de rigueur* Khaki uniform tie. "Scared me so bad I almost wet my pants. I flashed the light around down there looking for something white and thought I'd found the drawings but it wasn't them at all . . . it was a skull. A human skull, with a big hole in it. And it's still connected to the rest of the skeleton. Looks like somebody got bumped off quite a few years back and then was tossed in there to rot."

Bubba hunched down secretively and leaned a little closer to Poppy. "I'm pretty sure I know who it is . . . Zoe's not gonna be happy at all, but there's an old blue nylon backpack down there, too. On the name tag by one of those sixties peace symbols, it says *Ain't gonna study war no more — property of J.C. Hightower, Jr."*

Poppy sucked in air to make an appropriate comment but the words were lost as a great hollow *bloompp!!* of sound echoed all around them.

"Goddamn, son — that was a shot!" Poppy said, more calm than she felt, and then pulled Belle to her and hit the ground out of instinct as Bubba leaped toward the other women.

"Get down!" he shouted, and Zoe and Red did so, but Violet looked disdainfully at the muddy earth and chose instead to fling herself gracefully into the open back end of the Suburban, her furtop boots sticking out like kittens with muddy bellies.

158

The silence was broken only by the sounds of their own grunts and groans. After a few moments Bubba rose cautiously and said "Well, someone over there is shooting." He pointed across the valley, "But we don't seem to be the target."

The whizzing of knobby tires on mud and the humming roar of a carelessly revved engine announced the presence of a vehicle on the road leading to Bitsy Drake's studio. The sound came closer, then suddenly, like a black and silver buzzsaw spewing twin fishtails of red mud, Collin Drake's GMC pickup burst sliding from the woods and skidded to a crooked stop beside the workroom. Collin Drake was out of the truck and into the building as fast as any concerned and caring father. A moment later his long, loud anguished cry chilled Poppy's heart.

She sensed immediately what had happened. Bubba seemed to have figured it out also. He took charge of the situation, efficiently executing textbook technique in his immediate actions. He quickly made his way through the fence, across the two hundred yards or so, and cautiously entered the open doorway.

After a reassuring word to Belle and the other women, Poppy followed him, leaving them behind with no knowledge of what else Bubba had found in the well. She traced the young deputy's steps, entering the workroom and proceeding toward the sound of Collin Drake's hoarse sobbing.

Jesusmaryandjoseph. She did it in the birthday room! The scene was much worse than she could've imagined. Collin Drake was sitting on the floor, seemingly covered in blood. He was gibbering and vainly trying to replace his daughter's head on her

159

shoulders. Her neckbone had been completely blown away by a blast obviously delivered by a shotgun that was efficiently wired into the hands of a new figure across the room. A figure surely fashioned in the likeness of J.C. Junior.

Poppy grabbed Bubba who stood transfixed, sans technique, just inside the doorway. "You okay, son?" He blinked rapidly, and regained a little color. "Yeah . . . uuhhh." He cleared his throat and spoke in a surprisingly strong voice.

"Mr. Drake. Let me help you, sir." Bubba knelt beside the distraught man on the floor. Collin allowed Bubba to pull him away from his daughter's broken body.

Then Poppy saw the note.

It was impaled on one of the glass candles on the cake. She resisted the urge to clean her glasses before leaning close to read the darkly penciled words.

Im sorry Daddy I just cant live with it any more. What I have done is so awful. Too many people are dead because of me. Its all over now — they have found J.C. Im not worth your love and protection Please please forgive me I love you — Coleeta

Suddenly Collin Drake focused on Poppy. He seemed to direct the immensity of his rage and grief onto her slim form. "You! It's your fault! All you damned queers over there! Alway's suckin' around here — meddling! Keeping Coleeta stirred up. Askin' questions about that queer's coward little brother!"

He sucked in air and stared wild-eyed at Poppy. "I oughta *kill* you!"

He lunged for her, his long bloody arms outstretched. She neatly sidestepped him as he slipped on the blood-covered floor and fell hard against the door jamb. Bubba was on him quickly and secured Collin Drake's wrists together behind him with a decisive click of his handcuffs.

"You can't do that, sir," Bubba told him. "I've deputized Miz Dillworth." He shoved a badge at Poppy. "Drake, you're under arrest for threatening an officer of the law.'"

Poppy jabbed the pin on the shiny star into her jacket lapel and tried to swallow back a lump in her throat. Even in the midst of the physical and emotional chaos of the present moment, she was proudly conscious of the weight of the metal Sheriff's badge against her collarbone.

I made it, Irma. See, honey. I finally made it!

She helped Bubba perform the tasks she had seen others do for forty-five years during that other lifetime in the Caliche County Sheriff's Department.

Within a very few minutes, the Todo Rojo firehouse ambulance had been summoned. Bubba snipped the barbed wire fence and brought the big Suburban over to collect a now subdued but still seething Collin Drake. He stared balefully at Poppy as Bubba led him from the scene of his daughter's suicide.

"Coleeta wouldna ever killed anybody else if you people hadn't make her desperate!" He almost hissed at Poppy, his voice low and husky with loathing.

Bubba said quietly, "Miz Dillworth, would you please help complete our investigation in there before my daddy gets here and we lose our chance?" He handed Poppy his camera and a set of clear plastic bags, then led Collin Drake off to sit in the Suburban.

"Okay," she said to his retreating back. "But

would you tell Zoe and the rest what's happened? They should go on home and I'll meet them there later." She pointed at the five women lined up against the fence like curious birds. Red Swindell seemed especially agitated. *'Spose she finally figured out old Delbert's secret identity, after all?*

Poppy finished photographing Coleeta Drake's bloody body, her nausea threatening to overwhelm her. Her head was still attached to her body, but only barely, by the tendons and neck skin on the left side.

As Poppy heard the siren and horns of several vehicles nearing the studio, Bubba came to stand beside her in the doorway. She patted him quickly on the shoulder and braced herself for the arrival of Daddy Bert and his traveling circus.

— 16 —
A Big Girl's Closet

Poppy sat on the loveseat in front of Zoe's fireplace absently stroking Cleo, who'd somehow insinuated her warm grey length between Poppy's leg and Belle's. She mused silently about Bubba's grisly, surprising discovery of yesterday. So J.C. had never left the ranch. Bitsy's suicide note seemed to tie everything up in a neat little package.

Most everything.

But not *everything*, Poppy's intuition reminded her.

Bubba's daddy was happy with it all, though. Now the county wouldn't have the expense of a trial. Nan's death was still a suicide in the narrow confines of the sheriff's mind and on the county's books. Now with Coleeta Drake's macabre self-murder, he could happily stamp CASE CLOSED on Morgana's murder also. And, as he so less-than-charmingly put it, *the bungled barbecue at the guest house* would need no more of the county's precious time spent on it.

Comforting sounds of female laughter from Zoe and Marcie in the kitchen made Poppy aware once more of how happy she was. Belle dozed beside her, her head snuggled against Poppy's shoulder and her feet stretched out toward the glowing fire.

But some things kept bothering Poppy. Pertinent questions remained unanswered. Though Violet was now cleared of charges, Poppy couldn't make all her questions and suspicions go away. They bubbled to the top of her mind again and again, displacing the neatly fitting lid of Bitsy's suicide.

The laughter from the kitchen grew rowdier as Marcie bounced through the doorway, mock-chased by Zoe who looked appropriately domesticated with a pink, ruffled bib-apron double-wrapped around her rangy hips. She dried her long fingers on it while she spoke. "We got a wonderful idea."

Belle sat up straight beside Poppy and stretched, yawning, as Zoe continued. "How about we pack a picnic lunch and go for a horseback ride down to the bottoms where Marcie and I are gonna build our house?"

Poppy couldn't help but notice the sparkle this

suggestion brought to Belle's eyes. And for a moment Poppy actually considered going herself — but instead of eagerly agreeing, she heard herself saying, "I think it's a grand idea, but there are still a few things about this whole business that're really bothering me. Y'all go ahead." She smiled at Belle. "Yes, hon, you go on with them. I know you've been wanting to ride, and I need to talk to Violet about a few things that're stuck in my craw."

Belle hesitated briefly, casting a worried frown at Poppy, but gave in when Poppy prodded, "Unless you think you're too *old* to go prancing around on horseback, that is." She was a little ashamed of herself for manipulating Belle, but she really needed some time to herself to think.

The intensity of her new relationship kept distracting her mind from analytical chores. Right now what she really wanted to do was to shut off her bubbling brain and go off on holiday with the three women. The day was perfect, clear and bright. The sun's warmth had melted all but the most shaded places of the sleet and snow. The earth was drying rapidly as the breeze picked up from the west. A great day for a picnic with the woman she loved.

But. Yes, *but!* The puzzle wasn't solved. And until it was, Poppy wouldn't feel right. Too many questions yet to be answered. She smiled at Belle and the others, watching their excited preparations — again feeling the tug to go with them — but heeded instead the call of duty and said, "Before you do, will you help me with some sleuthing?"

After a chorus of yeses, they sat around the kitchen table and watched expectantly as Poppy smoothed out a piece of paper and sharpened a

165

pencil. "I need your brains for a little while." She tapped the paper with the pencil eraser. "These are all the questions I've come up with since we got here, Marcie. I want to run through them and see if the Bitsy-done-it theory works with all of them."

Poppy cleaned her spectacles and plopped them decisively on her nose. "Number one. Why did Nan go to the bluff? She must've gone there to meet someone. Was she tricked into going? Wouldn't she have recognized Bitsy's voice if Bitsy called her — and why meet there? Doesn't make much sense, does it?"

Zoe spoke up first. "Well, no, it doesn't. But, Bitsy *must*'ve done it. She must've killed J.C. all those years ago and kept the pistol and shot Nan with it. I have to admit it does puzzle me why Nan went to the bluff though. If it'd been her own idea, I think she'd have ridden her horse up there. Someone must've called. And then too, Nan had made the appointment to meet Cletus Barnes in Dallas later that morning. She clearly didn't intend to waste time."

Marcie said, "Maybe Bitsy promised to tell her something about J.C.'s whereabouts."

"It probably was somethin' like that, but I still can't figure out why Bitsy would've chosen the bluff as a place to meet. Why wouldn't she have asked Nan to meet her at her house or at the studio?" Poppy rubbed absently at one lens of her glasses.

Belle offered, "Suppose she didn't want Collin to know about it?" Then answered her own question. "But, then she'd have just had Nan come down to the guest house to meet her there."

166

"I guess the only one who could've told us the answer to that is dead," Zoe said with finality.

"I'm not so sure about that," Poppy said stubbornly. "That's why it's number one on my list of unanswered questions."

She made a few cryptic pencil marks on the paper before her, then continued. "Number two. Who tampered with the jeep's brakes the day we went to town? It doesn't fit with anything we know about either Bitsy's capabilities or her habits."

"Yeah . . ." Zoe looked thoughtful then said, "I'll betcha Collin followed us to town that day and did it himself as a warning for us to keep away from Bitsy. Remember, he saw us when Marcie took the video pictures of his place."

"One helluva strong warning. Coulda killed us all," Poppy answered. "But, I agree that it had to be Collin Drake that did it. As long as J.C. was a viable suspect, I thought he or a friend of his had done it. Remember the big Mercedes truck that passed us on the way to Collin's that day? Well later, in town, after we met Bubba and Red at the cafe, I saw the truck at that Fina station close to the square. The driver was a long-haired fellow that certainly could have been the rumored J.C."

Cleo, who'd been ignored just long enough to actively seek attention, stood on her hind legs and placed two silky front paws on Poppy's thigh. Belle quickly picked her up and held her while Poppy continued speaking.

"Now that we know J.C. was never a live suspect, well . . . that changes everything in my mind, at least. But, I still can't buy the pat solution that

Bubba's daddy is pushing. Maybe, just maybe, Bitsy did kill J.C. and kept the gun — but I still keep rassling with the purpose of the second shot fired out of that pistol. And besides — we really don't know, until Bubba gets the forensics report on that skull from the well, whether or not that old pistol was actually what killed J.C."

Not to be denied, Cleo leaped into Poppy's lap and swished her feathered tail in front of Poppy's eyes.

Face it, Wondercrone — the sybaritic little furball has a crush on you!

Poppy laughed, gathered Cleo against her shoulder and stroked her gleaming fur. This action prompted a loud fit of uninhibited purring from the happy cat and effectively ended the question-and-answer session at the table.

"Well, anyhow," Poppy concluded, over Cleo's slurpy rumbling. "You all go on and get some fresh air and me and my new partner here will stay and tie up some loose ends." Cleo opened her almond eyes right on cue and meowed in seeming agreement.

The others dressed and packed their lunch as Poppy and Cleo sat before the fire. Poppy stared at the paper in her hand without really seeing it. For various reasons she hadn't voiced several points that still puzzled her, the first one being that everyone just assumed that Bitsy Drake's note was a confession to *everything*. It did seem possible now to Poppy that Bitsy *could* have killed J.C. and maybe Morgana, but the cold, calculated shooting of Nan Hightower just didn't fit with the craziness of the other two murders.

Zoe seemed willing to accept the idea that Coleeta Drake had killed Nan, but Poppy couldn't buy it. It also occurred to Poppy that she really didn't know Nan Hightower, except through the descriptions and stories of others. She felt a sudden need to see where Nan had lived, to see Nan's room at the ranch house, to get a feeling of who the woman had really been.

She hugged Belle and kissed her, and was momentarily overcome with a passionate regret that she wasn't going with them. Then she urged Belle to be careful — to come back to her safely — and then turned quickly toward the phone, the questioning sentences for Violet already forming in her mind as her ears registered the laughter of the women walking toward the stable.

* * * * *

A few minutes later, still holding a smugly happy Cleo, Poppy paused on the path beside the glistening azure pool behind the ranch house and waved to her friends as they rode away. Violet had readily agreed to Poppy's request and Lupe opened the back door for her before her finger left the doorbell.

"*Buenas dias*, Miss Poppy. And to you too, *mi belleza. Gatita grande.* Come to Lupe." She extended her arms toward Cleo who obligingly let herself be lifted from Poppy's grasp and carried like a baby in the makeshift hammock of Lupe's yellow apron.

Poppy followed Lupe past the goldfish pool in the sunny atrium and down a hallway that branched off from the one to Violet's suite. The pronounced contrast between the seemingly masculine bedroom they entered and the ultra-feminine opulence of Violet's boudoir struck Poppy as almost purposeful in the completeness of its differing.

Every wall was a mirror. Except for the open spaces of wide picture windows on one wall where Poppy looked out onto a carefully landscaped, walled courtyard, the room was a kaleidoscope of reflected images. The startling effect was of a room with no walls at all. Surprisingly the ceiling wasn't mirrored, although it opened into two immense octagonal skylights. The ceiling itself was heavily troweled, off-white stucco. A king-size, four-poster bed of dark, carved wood was the centerpiece of the room. A spread of tanned zebra skin dropped unevenly to the floor on both sides of it.

Poppy was barely aware of Lupe closing the door as she left and of Cleo leaning against her ankles as she stood rooted in the center of the carmine and black carpet. She turned to see a wide doorway that opened onto the bathroom. The gleam of chrome was evident, even without the lights switched on.

An open archway to the left disclosed shadowy rows of garments hanging in regimented groups. Poppy entered the gloom of the large closet and pressed a button she supposed to be a light switch. Her heart leaped as the ranks of clothing marched suddenly toward her, then stopped and swayed lightly. She giggled suddenly as her fear dissipated before a silly mental image of the swaying elephants from Disney's *Fantasia*.

She pressed another button and this time light flooded the room, illuminating the fact that easily one half of the garments were made of leather.

Yeppers! This lesbiggie shore had a thang for leather. 'Nuff dead animal skins in here to prompt a protest from a hard-case Neiman-Marcus fur junkie!

Poppy's irreverent inner voice was snuffed into silence as her gaze fell on a row of exquisite, paired, tooled-leather cowboy boots. All black. Every last pointed toe and stacked heel was jet-coal-obsidian, unforgiving black-hole black.

Whoa up here, Fearless Tracker. Warn't no boots in that box the no-neck pisser showed us down at the sheriff's office.

She walked quickly back to the main doorway, studied the bank of buttons beside it and finally pressed one marked *kitchen*. She was rewarded almost immediately by Lupe's lilting answering voice. "Yes, Miss Poppy. Are you needing something?"

Poppy pressed the *speak* button and asked, "Can you come here for a minute, Lupe? I need to ask you a question."

A slight buzzing ensued from the speaker above the door as Lupe apparently considered the request, then a reticent voice came back. *"Yes. Okay. . . . I am coming."*

A few moments later the door opened softly and Lupe's white head appeared around the door jamb.

"Come on in, Lupe. I won't bite . . . I promise."

The door opened fully and the nervous woman entered, drying un-wet hands on her apron.

"Can you tell me which boots Nan was wearing the day she died? Are they here in the closet?"

Lupe's blue-veined hands flew to her face. "Yes. The sheriff — he gave them to me. I put them with the others. I have done no wrong to them, have I, Miss Poppy? The sheriff, he said he was through with the boots, so I cleaned and polished them." Her white brows met over her nose in a worried frown.

171

"No, Lupe. You did just right. Don't fret. I just want to see which pair she was wearing." Poppy gently took Lupe's arm and moved toward the closet.

"These are the ones here. Her newest boots. She only just bought them before she . . . before she . . . passed away." Lupe pointed to the first pair in line. Stovepipe tops, straight cut with a distinct Spanish flair to the stitching. Poppy picked up one and turned it to the light. Just the tiniest of wear marks appeared on the tough shiny smoothness of the toe. She lifted it to her nose and sniffed the inside. Definitely *new* boots. She turned to Lupe who still stood in the closet doorway. "How often did Ms. Hightower buy new boots?"

"Oh, every year. She always buys a whole new set of clothes *every* autumn. Ever since she was a little girl it is her habit to get all new things to wear. Like for school." Lupe's face brightened at the memory, then saddened again as she remembered why Poppy had asked the question. "She always keeps some older pairs of boots — but everything else she always gives away to the Goodwill when she buys her new things. Such a waste of money but she always laughs and says not to worry. That black oil from the ground will pay for new black leather for her body. She is . . . she *was* very peculiar in that way."

"Thank you, Lupe. You've been very helpful." Poppy dismissed the old woman with a pat on her arm and she walked quickly toward the door.

"Oh, Lupe. I forgot to ask about the gloves she wore that day. Did she always buy new gloves also?"

Lupe turned and answered without hesitation. "Oh si — always new gloves too. When she was a little girl I had to make her take them off to sleep.

172

She loved to make a fist, like so." Lupe fisted her hand, then flexed and fisted again. "The sheriff did not give me any gloves, but Miss Nancy must have worn her *new* ones. She always keeps an old pair in her trunk for problems — but I cannot think she would go off in new boots without new gloves."

"Thanks, Lupe. Thank you very much." Poppy turned back toward the closet as Lupe closed the door. Cleo, who'd been conducting her own investigation of the Hightower digs, took this moment to sharpen her claws on the cantle of an ancient leather-and-wood saddle underneath a rack of chrome and glass that served as a bedside stand. She got in a number of quick stab-pulls before Poppy lifted her gently away from it.

"C'mere, you old ratter," she said into the deep fur of Cleo's neck as she carried the cat to the window. "Did you hear *that,* Miss Kitty? *Abuela* Lupe says *new* gloves. But no-neck pisser showed Mama Mariposa *old* gloves! What you think of that, hummm?" Cleo's answering purr escalated to Evinrude level as Poppy nuzzled her neck.

Y'know, Papillon — old mariposa — for an "out" dog-woman, you're showin' definite signs of fe-licitous behavior here.

173

– 17 –
Thundering Hoofbeats

Poppy returned to the cabin with Cleo and fixed them both some lunch. Sardines and crackers. No crackers for Cleo, of course. Poppy munched and fought off crumbs as the VCR *click-clacked* in response to the remote control she pointed at it. One more time she watched Zoe and Marcie re-enact the whole scene of Nan's death on the bluff.

She jumped at the shrill ring of the phone, impatiently punched the *pause* button on the control, then rose and answered it. "Hello. Zoe isn't here. This is Poppy Dillworth speaking . . . Oh, hi Bubba."

Bubba's troubled voice rose as he spoke to Poppy. "Daddy let Collin out of jail and he's over at the funeral home now, making arrangements to cremate his daughter's remains. I still think there's something dead wrong about him. I'm comin' out to his place to look around."

Poppy answered with concern, "Yeah — I've got some problems with this whole thing too. I just found out Nan was wearing new gloves when she left home the morning she was killed, but the gloves in your evidence box are old and worn out." Poppy was suddenly aware of the hair lifting slightly on her neck.

"Well, it took a lot of some kind of flammable liquid to start the fire at the guest house, and there weren't any empty cans at Bitsy's studio. I wanna look around Collin's place before he gets back out there."

"Be careful, son," Poppy said quietly. "You hear?"

"Yes, ma'am, I hear. I'll watch out, but in case anything happens to me . . . well, Red has copies of all my notes on this case."

"Okay." Poppy swallowed against a sudden constriction in her throat. "Let me know what you find."

"All right. I'll call when I get back to town."

Poppy cradled the receiver and turned again toward the flickering television screen where a crow hovered in frozen flight above a sawed-off fencepost.

Sawed-off?

The hair on her neck went into a full, terpsichorean two-step as the implications of what she was seeing sunk in.

Of course, Dillworth, you dipshit! It ain't the crow at all. It's the friggin' fencepost that keeps comin' to mind!

She looked again at the screen, then rewound the tape for a few seconds and watched it again in slow motion. Sure enough. She hadn't seen the shorter fencepost before because the crow was perched on it. Then when the crow flew away, her eye had followed the bird's movement.

Poppy *knew* it was important.

Somehow.

But how?

Why would Collin Drake have recently sawed off the top ten inches or so from a large corner post next to his barn? Her eye traveled over the scene still flickering on the screen. The rest of the buildings and fencing were a uniform, paintless gray. Some of the other posts were crooked or split and weathered, but none of them had been repaired or cut off neatly at the top. Only one. The new wood grain of the fresh cut flashed bright yellow as the crow lifted forward, up and away from it.

She clicked the picture forward and stopped it as Collin Drake passed jerkily behind the post toward the house. She stopped it when he turned toward them and frowned. She studied the face of a man who didn't realize his picture was being taken, his thin, angular face fierce in a display of open hatred.

Poppy shivered, picked up Cleo and held her close.

She clicked off the frightening image, laid the remote control on the coffee table and sat for a few moments smoothing her hand down Cleo's soft back and sides.

Maybe she ought to get on over there. Give Bubba a hand. Just in case Collin came back from town early before Bubba finished snooping.

She spent a few seconds searching for the keys to Zoe's jeep, then spied them hanging on a pegged board beside the front door. She removed them quickly, a fluttery sense of urgency propelling her from the cabin and into the vehicle.

Poppy barely registered Cleo's arch observation from her protested exile in the cabin window. Her mind was on the pieces to the puzzle. The pieces that should fit but didn't. The weight of her pistol in her vest pocket bumped reassuringly against her side as she drove the jeep over the ranch roads past the bluff where Nan had been killed and onto the road that led to Collin Drake's place.

She let out a sigh of relief as she neared the house and saw only Collin's GMC in the drive. Good. Bubba either wasn't there yet or had come and gone. Maybe she was overreacting. She'd recognized raw hatred on Drake's face on the video. But perhaps a father was allowed to show frustration and anger toward those he saw as threatening to his daughter.

She pulled the jeep up close to the barns and honked the horn. No sense getting run off or yelled at, or worse, if she could help it. She honked again but nothing stirred. Not even a face at a window. She turned off the engine and listened to the stillness. It seemed she heard the hum of a vehicle from back toward the river, but it could easily be coming across the fields from the highway. The older she got, the harder it was to discern the direction of sound.

The ground gave spongily beneath her boots as she stepped cautiously from the jeep. The wind was completely still and the warmth of the sun made the day seem like Indian summer. Far off *honk-onks* of a great flying wedge of Canadian geese caught her attention, and for a moment she watched the long straggling vee open and close, rippling against the cobalt sky.

She cupped her hands and *halooed* at the house. Just in case. Still no answer. She walked to the post with the newly cut top and examined it. The yellow and gold of freshly cut, seasoned *bois d'arc* wood shined up at her. The side of the post that faced the barn was splintered down a bit, past the cut, toward the ground. A few long slivers had been pulled away. Maybe the cut hadn't gone all the way through and it pulled away when the top fell off. Or was taken off.

She couldn't get as close to the post as she wanted from where she stood on the outside of the fence because of a thick mass of cactus at the base of it. She went through the open gateway and stood facing the other side.

No. The cut was clean. All the way across the top. The splinters had been there before the top was sawed off. What could've happened to the strong, old, fine-grained *bois d'arc* post that would cause it to shatter, or split like that on the top? And why cut it off? As long as the fence wires were still tight, why bother to remove the splintered top? The barbed wire zinged and hummed tautly in answer to Poppy's inquisitive touch.

She looked toward the house, half expecting Collin Drake to burst from the door at any moment. Her gaze traveled over the yard toward the back porch. Suddenly the woodpile claimed her attention. A half moon of yellow winked back at her from the neatly stacked firewood. She walked excitedly toward it.

Well, diddly damn, Dillworth. Lookee here!

She gingerly moved a few lengths of firewood, uncovering the piece of shattered post. She turned it with her boot until the splintered side faced up, then rolled it over until it faced up again and discovered what she'd known she would find. A hole about the size of a dime. Or a bullet. A .45 caliber bullet that had entered but did not leave the block of wood at her feet.

She carefully grasped the piece by the edges, carried it back to the post and turned it to fit. It dropped neatly into place.

Someone had stood where she was standing and had, with the left hand, fired a large caliber pistol at the post. Had to be that way — the cactus was in the way on the other side. Or maybe it had been a rifle? No. That made no sense. Not enough room between the barn wall and the post for anyone to fire a rifle from that direction.

Poppy's excited attention centered next on the barn. The barn Collin had come from that day. She stepped into the gloom of the large building, trying to adjust her eyes to the shadows. She gathered her courage and flipped a light switch beside the door.

The cavernous room was dark in the upper

reaches. The area illuminated by a single, wire-suspended light bulb was full of clutter. Old farm machinery, tools and stacks of water-stained cardboard boxes lined the corner where she stood. One of four large red fuel cans lay on the dirt floor, as if dropped by someone — not simply toppled from the stack.

She looked closer at the ground. It was scuffed with deep sliding footprints. Then she saw something that sent her cardiac leprechaun into an arrhythmic fit. A snippet of khaki cloth hung limply from a nail that protruded from the supporting center-post near where the can marked KEROSENE lay on the ground. And two long furrows pointed toward the doorway. The kind of marks that boot heels or shoes would make if someone was dragged.

Bubba! Goddamn. The sumbitch got the boy!

Poppy stood perfectly still for a moment and made her lungs draw three long, slow breaths while she looked carefully around her. Satisfied the men were not still in the barn, she flipped off the switch and walked cautiously out into the daylight.

Jesusmaryandjoseph!

Panic flowed in waves, curling at her feet as she struggled to wade free.

Shut up, you old fool. Think! She squelched her inner confusion and turned decisively toward the jeep and saw the very *worst* thing she could ever possibly see. Toward the river a stream of gray smoke rose lazily into the still sky. Smoke from the kilns at Bitsy's studio. Dead Bitsy . . . Live Collin . . .

Live Bubba?

She looked down as she planted her foot, readying herself for the upward lunge into the driver's seat. There on the ground beside her boot was the

180

peculiar, deep signature tread mark of Bubba's Suburban. A row of little red clay diamonds crumbled against her boot as she wavered, one foot on the step-up and one on the ground.

The seat springs recoiled against her backside as she bounced into the vehicle. The tire marks continued down the road in the direction of the studio. The studio where smoke rose steadily from a dead woman's ovens.

Poppy started the jeep, spun it around and headed off, following the tracks of Bubba's vehicle toward the smoke. Her heart drummed a rickety tattoo now as her fears began to take form in her imagination.

Collin must've surprised the young deputy in the barn and gotten the drop on him. She remembered the two straight furrows in the dry dirt of the barn floor. *And dragged him out? Yeah . . . had to be out cold or he'da been throwing his feet around.* A cold knot of fear settled in her abdomen as she ground the little jeep through its gears, driving as if the distance to the studio were the last mile of the LeMans.

As she skidded past a pond, ducks scattered, running little topwater races of their own as they struggled to lift into flight. A sudden squeeze of caution brought her foot off the accelerator. The jeep slowed just before the last rise between her and the studio. She stopped, killed the engine, and sat very still — listening.

Nothing. No sound came from over the hill — nothing moved except the silent smoke. She was just about to sneak the rest of the way on foot when she heard an engine start up. It had to be Bubba's Suburban. The low, smooth rumble of the big engine was familiar. The sound seemed to be moving away from her, away and down — toward the river.

She made her decision. The boy was either okay or he wasn't. And if he wasn't, he was probably getting more un-okay by the second. No time to waste. The little engine sprang to life, and she sped up and over the hill just in time to catch a glimpse of Bubba's Chevy lumbering slowly into the woods toward the river.

Poppy's heart leaped in imitation of relief. She wanted to think Bubba was in the vehicle, but her intuition wouldn't allow it.

No . . . no . . . NO! You know where he is. Get him out, woman! GET HIM OUT!

She side-skidded the jeep up beside the outside kiln and hit the ground running. The firebox was stuffed crazily, sticks and flitches of wood haphazardly crammed into it. Fire glowed red through the narrow opening where it hadn't been properly shut.

Burning wood scattered as Poppy scraped wildly at the firebox, digging out the embers with a small shovel that had been leaning against the woodpile. She cleared all she could and burned her hands as she slapped at a smoldering hole in the knee of her jeans. *Okay. That's done! Now get'im out!*

The heavy handle of the kiln's metal door wouldn't budge. She looked desperately for something to turn the long handle with and spied a rusty bar by the studio. She kicked aside the still-burning wood and wedged the bar under the handle, levering it up.

Sumbitch! You bastard! You open, goddamn you!

It didn't.

She pulled the bar loose, lodged it over the handle

and swung her weight against it, reversing the direction of the leverage. The bar bent slowly but the door remained tightly shut.

Tears of frustration and pain squeezed from the corners of her eyes as her back muscles screamed in revolt.

A cold fury enveloped her. In spite of it, she felt an almost eerie inner calm of pure determination. Her brain supplied the answer even before her anxious gaze fell on the jeep.

The winch cable!

Her hands performed the necessary strenuous task of manually releasing the press-lock on the cable spool, though on some level of consciousness she knew she was pushing her aging body across boundaries set up years ago.

She unreeled the steel cable toward the door, dropped the hook securely over the handle, and raced back to the jeep and started it.

Slow girl — slow — don't pop it!

The cable rose tautly into the air as she backed smoothly away. She lightly pressed the gas pedal. *A little more, just a little more . . . The wheels grabbed the ground hard and the cable sang as the vehicle inched away.*

Zziiiinnnggg! The cable whipped into the air and the jeep leaped backward as the handle gave way.

"Yaahoo!" She tumbled from the seat and ran for the door of the kiln. She could hardly believe her eyes as she knelt in front of it. The handle had broken cleanly away from the still closed door.

Ohmygod. Her heart pounded as disappointment gave way to another furious surge of inspiration. She ran back to the jeep, stood and stretched tall from

the step-up bar, and took a visual bead on her target
— a beehive of hot bricks with a young man inside.

She sat calmly and drove unswerving toward the
kiln. The front bumper tapped it lightly. She backed
up a few feet, then cannoned forward. The jeep hit
the brick kiln with a bone-crunching jolt. She wiped
the dust, sweat and tears away from her straining
eyes to discover a jagged crack had appeared. Back
she went. Forward. *Crash!*

Back.

CRUNCH!

Take that you bastard!

Back again.

CRASH!

Not gonna beat me, you . . .

Back . . .

Courses of bricks crumbled inward and dust rose
into the air as the kiln finally gave way to Poppy's
insistent battering. She bounded from the jeep and
clambered into the rubble, looking desperately for
Bubba. Her foot struck something soft.

Please-oh-please be alive! She tugged and pushed
the heavy bricks away from the body of the young
man. She realized then that the inside of the kiln
was only warm. Not hot. Maybe he was okay, maybe
he —

Unnnhhh." A muffled groan rose from deep in his
chest.

ALIVE!

Poppy scraped and pushed furiously at the
remaining bricks and freed Bubba from beneath them.
His head was sticky-red under the dust and his left
arm twisted away from his shoulder at an unnatural

angle. His wrists were bound together in front of him with his own handcuffs.

Get'im in the jeep. Got to get'im some help.

She looked back at the vehicle and her hammering heart stuttered as she saw the left front wheel was leaning inward, jammed against the wheel well. The last juggernaut action had crippled their only means of escape.

She looked frantically around her, searching for some clue of what to do next. Then she saw him. A movement down the road where the Suburban had disappeared. A man walking. Collin Drake. She watched, motionless, as he stopped, brought a hand up to shade his face and looked up at the studio. Then he abruptly began a clumsy trot toward them.

Poppy got her arms under Bubba's and locked her hands around his narrow chest. For the second time in less than an hour, an unconscious Bubba was transported with the heels of his Tony Lamas plowing the red dirt.

The door to the studio was locked. Poppy pulled the ring of metal picks free from her pocket and quickly located the correct one. Two seconds, no less, and the door swung open. She pulled Bubba inside and laid him, broken and bloody, along the wall, then shut and locked the door and jammed a pick into the lock from the inside, leaving the whole ring of metal picks hanging from the door.

She allowed herself a quick look to see where Collin was, and groaned as she saw him come to a panting stop by the ruined kiln. He leaned forward and grasped his thighs with rangy hands, heaving from the effects of his uphill run.

185

The sun glinted off something in his hip pocket. As he moved it flashed again and Poppy saw with despair it was Bubba's nickel-plated .357 Magnum. She tugged at the weight of her own pistol in her vest pocket, assuring herself of its reality as she moved toward the telephone by the door.

She dialed zero and caught her breath as she heard Collin cursing at the door. The ring of picks swayed as he tried to use his key in the lock. Poppy jumped as he bellowed in frustration and kicked his heavy boots against the unyielding door.

The operator answered. "May I help you?"

"This is an emergency. I don't have a phone book. Connect me with the Rojo County Sheriff's Office. Bubba Swindell's been injured!"

"Yes ma'am, rightaway," the pleasant male voice assured her.

Poppy listened, desperately wishing for the 911 service of larger cities. The number rang three times before the thready voice of Pappy Swindell came on. "County Sheriff."

"Pappy — this is Poppy Dillworth! I'm at —" She stopped speaking. The line had gone dead. No sound at all came from the receiver. She pressed the square button rapidly in a futile attempt to raise an answer. The knot in her stomach tightened.

She knew what must have happened. Collin had cut the phone line. Habit directed her hand as she replaced the useless receiver on the hook. She dropped to the floor and crawled toward Bubba's inert form, where he lay along the wall beneath the window.

Just as she reached him, the lower panes of the window exploded inward with a ballooning crash of

186

stinging, flying glass. She rolled to her back and pulled her small .38 from her pocket. She unsnapped the holster and slid it carefully down and off the barrel and waited tensely for whatever was going to happen next.

She didn't have long to wait. The creased top of Collin Drake's black western hat rose slowly into view. Poppy raised her pistol and centered the notched sight exactly on the grosgrain hatband. She tightened her finger against the trigger.

The hat dipped slightly to one side as part of the wide brim appeared above the window ledge. Just as she realized the hat was atop a stick, Collin Drake's gloved fist bashed in another window pane along the bottom row.

Glass showered in on her, clicking off her spectacle lenses and stinging the hand that held the pistol. She rolled away, pulled her body to a cautious standing crouch behind the door, and watched the window warily. Collin, bolder now, was hunkered down outside beneath the opening. This was her chance to scare him off and buy them some precious time. Poppy raised the pistol and unhesitatingly fired at the only part of him she could get a bead on. His hip pocket and back belt loops.

The crashing echo of the shot rocketed off the inside walls of the concrete block building and left Poppy momentarily deafened. She heard through ringing ears the screeching curses of the wounded madman outside.

She surveyed her surroundings, employing the linear-think talent that would have made her a match for the great lawmen of all time if she'd ever had a chance, before now, to prove herself.

She swiftly covered the still-manacled Bubba with a dropcloth, then duckwalked, below the window level, across to the birthday room where fifty-pound bags of powdered, terra-cotta clay were stacked in waist-high rows beside the door. An open padlock hung from a hasp on the outside of the doorjamb. The Goddess had finally smiled. Poppy opened the door and switched on the light, then crawled back to the other side of the larger workroom toward a tableau Bitsy had been working on. A grouping of figures representing the French revolution.

She removed the gray wig and shawl from the figure of an old woman who sat knitting in a rocking chair. Madame DeFarge? She swiftly removed the figure, pushed it out of sight and took her place in the chair. She donned the wig, secured the shawl around her shoulders and placed the knitting basket in her lap. She gripped her pistol firmly beneath a hank of yarn. Her back was to the wall and from where she sat, she could see all the windows and doors.

She waited.

The quiet outside grew ominous. She breathed slowly, trying not to hyperventilate. Dizziness and numbness in her arms was something she could do without.

She flinched and sucked in a quick lungful of air. The outer door exploded open in a roaring flash of light, sound and splinters as Collin Drake shot out the lock and pulled the door open wide. He burst through the doorway, bobbing and weaving, turning wildly, peering into the gloom of the large room. She hoped to all the heavens that Bubba would remain still and quiet long enough for her plan to work.

As Drake's maddened gaze swept over her, the leprechaun froze in her chest. Her heart sat still for a moment, then leaped and pounded as the floodgates opened and blood rushed outward again, to lungs and brain.

He looked past her, unseeing, then back again. Then he spied the open door of the windowless birthday room. He tiptoed cautiously toward it, then dropped to his skinny haunches and leapfrogged into the lit room.

Poppy moved quickly. She willed her stiff knees to the doorway, slammed it shut and coolly clicked the padlock closed over the hasp. Then she began to furiously pile the heavy bags of clay against the door. Heaving and panting, she piled bag after bag of powdery clay, imprisoning the now thoroughly crazed Collin Drake.

He beat and kicked the door, hoarsely screaming obscenities. Then he was quiet for a few seconds and began, Poppy guessed, to destroy each of the figures in the room. The grinding crashes continued for a long moment, then the sound of great breathless sobs came from behind the door.

Then silence.

Poppy slid down the wall and sat beside Bubba who had begun to stir beneath the heavy white cloth. She peeled it back to give him some air. He moaned and struggled to sit.

"No, no, son. Stay put. Don't move." She leaned close to him. "It's me . . . Poppy. I'm here with you. Can you talk? Do you hear me?"

"Uunnnhh . . ." He croaked in pain as he tried to move, then ceased to struggle and said weakly, "Poppy? . . . Zat you? . . . Where's Drake?"

189

"I've got'im captured in Bitsy's birthday room. He's crazy as a loon. Busted in here shootin'. What'd he do to *you* anyhow?"

"Don't know. Knocked me out I guess . . . but he bragged. Told me everything. How he killed Miz Hightower and Morgana." Bubba's voice trailed off and he seemed about to pass out again.

Poppy grasped his shoulder gently but firmly. "Bubba, you got a walkie-talkie on your belt? Phone? *Anything?* Nobody knows we're here. Gotta get help."

A movement behind the stacks of clay bags claimed Poppy's attention as Bubba moaned at her side. Drake had finally calmed enough to think and had simply turned the doorknob and used brute strength to push the door open a crack until it stopped against the flat steel flap held in place by the padlock. Poppy watched in horror as the gleaming barrel of a pistol snaked out and rested its mouth against the lock.

Bloommmmpp!! The ruptured padlock clattered to the floor. Bags began to slip from the pile as Drake lunged against the door from the other side.

Poppy jerked in surprise as Bubba grasped her arm and spoke. "Miz Dillworth? Ma'am? I got his confession on tape. All he said when he was braggin' . . . unnnh . . ." His hands fell away, then found her arm again. "You're gonna hafta stop 'im. You're a deputy, remember . . . Protect . . . fellow officer . . ." His hands fell limply away as unconsciousness claimed him.

Poppy took a deep breath and stood, steadying her knees and legs beneath her. The crack of the door widened to about a foot and then opened out wider as the last of the bags tumbled to the floor. Poppy raised her pistol in front of her, held it firmly with both hands. As Collin Drake rushed screaming through the doorway toward her, she fired three rapid shots into his upper body. He fell forward, crumpling like the figures he knocked aside.

She watched incredulously, holding her breath as Drake raised Bubba's big pistol and pointed it at her. She squeezed the trigger of her .38 again and a dark hole appeared in the exact middle of his forehead. His head jerked back, then slammed face down against the layer of powdery clay beneath him.

Poppy lowered her pistol and felt her body start to sag toward the floor when she saw the blur of movement from the doorway. She felt Zoe's strong arms guide her out into the sunlight. She realized immediately what had happened, that her friends had heard the shots or seen the smoke and ridden across the bottoms to help. Poppy could see Zoe's lips moving but her shot-deafened ears weren't receiving a word. Then Belle had her around the waist and was covering her face with kisses.

Poppy sat cross-legged on the ground, then leaned against the wall as her hearing unfuzzed. She focused her scratchy eyes on Marcie who stood holding the reins of three very tired, froth-flecked horses.

Her stomach churned as the realization that she'd just killed a man claimed her. The waste of it, the ending of a human life . . . But the rush of emotion at knowing she'd had the guts to do what had to be done.

All her life she had wondered.

Now she knew.

Somewhere, rising incongruously through Poppy's distress, from way back in the outposts of her memory, a voice pushed its way through the years of clutter and intoned a familiar litany from childhood. Accompanied, of course, by galloping hoofbeats and the faraway strains of the William Tell Overture. *"Who was that masked man anyway, Ma?"*

And then she wept. Great gulping painful sobs racked her exhausted body as Belle hugged her close.

– 18 –
A Dead Man Speaks

Poppy moved slowly, ducking her head into the cold wind, lifting her aching knees gingerly up one step at a time, as she and Belle climbed the staired front walk of Rojo County's only hospital, Hand of God Presbyterian. It had been two whole days since the ugly scene at Coleeta Drake's studio, but Poppy's muscles and joints still made her painfully conscious of the punishing degree of their misuse.

Poppy and Belle rested for a moment on a sunny

bench in a red brick grotto outside the main door, protected from the biting wind. Poppy's eyes idly scanned a statue of Jesus whose outstretched left hand wore an aluminum pulltab on its ring finger. *Finally made the big commitment, huh fella?*

She rubbed her aching hands over her throbbing knees and looked up at the front of the hospital, where Bubba and his wife waited for them in room 324. Poppy fervently hoped the Hand of God had an elevator.

Her thoughts flitted back to the scene at the studio when Bubba's father and grandfather had arrived, and the satisfaction she'd received from telling them that "the boy" had been right all along. He had really clinched the case with his recording of Collin Drake's bragging confession, which Poppy and Belle were on their way now to hear for the first time.

Belle interrupted Poppy's musings. "Come back, Little Sheba. Earth-to-Dillworth . . . come in please."

Poppy grinned and faced her. "Sorry — I kinda took an ether trip, didn't I?" She'd felt strangely quiet since the traumatic shootout. Life — every tiny moment of it — was all the sweeter from having come so close to death. She suppressed a groan as she pushed herself off the bench and steadied her legs under her. "Onward and upward."

A small Christmas tree in the lobby winked at them as they sought out the elevator. Poppy calculated the date and realized with surprise that there were still two weeks left before the holiday. The past seven days at Red Rook Ranch seemed like a lifetime.

Their destination was at the end of a long hall

194

full of mostly open doorways. Voices of visitors and television game shows droned over them as they made their way to Bubba's room.

He was sitting up in bed, thin inside the loose-fitting hospital pajamas. His left arm was captured in an L-shaped cast held out from his body by a brace, and the whole top of his head was neatly swathed, mummy-like, in ribbons of white gauze. He smiled when he spied Poppy and Belle in the doorway. Red Swindell was sitting on Bubba's bed with one leg dangling while she hugged his knees. She scrambled to her feet as the two older women entered the room.

After warm greetings and awkward hugs, Bubba, with Red's help, got right to the other reason for the visit. Red closed the door and they sat silently listening to the slim little pocket recorder in Bubba's good hand.

A scratchy roar of engine noise filled the room as the tiny tape spools began to move. Then Bubba's recorded voice — *"You're gonna kill me, aren't you Collin?"*

"Of course I'm gonna kill you . . . you don't think I'm stupid, do you?

"No . . . I think you must be pretty smart. I can't figure out how you killed Nan Hightower and made it look like a suicide."

"Oh, that was easy . . . guess it cain't hurt to tell you that — since you ain't gonna live to tell it anyhow."

Red Swindell's already pale face grew even whiter as Collin Drake's chilling voice continued.

"I lifted her gloves out of her pickup one day in town. I'd been figurin' on the whole scheme for a

while. Ever since she started pokin' around askin' questions about her no-good bastard of a brother . . . 'Course I had the gun. Ever since I took it away from Bitsy the night she shot that sonuvabitch, almost twenty years ago."

Collin's voice paused and the roar of an engine sounded louder as he evidently maneuvered the big Chevy over a tricky stretch of road.

Bubba's voice came next, prompting. *"If you're so smart, how come you didn't fill in that old well?"*

"That's it . . . that's the one thing I never knew." The voice on the tape lowered with emotion, sorrow, Poppy thought. *"I knew Bitsy'd killed him . . . Found her wanderin' up the road that night, pistol in her hand, but she never told me what she did with the body. When she wanted me to build her that place down there, I figured she musta dumped him in the river that night. You're right . . . if I'd known that fucker was in the well this whole thing wouldna got so messy!"* Collin Drake's voice trailed off.

"How come you stole Miz Hightower's gloves?" Bubba's voice again, picking and pulling the story from him.

"The queer bitch was left-handed. That's why . . . you don't get it yet, do you, Swindell. You're dumber'n your daddy, ain'tcha?"

Poppy noticed Red Swindell's orange brows had come together. Tiny jerks beside her ear betrayed the tightness of her jaw.

Bubba's taped voice persisted. *"Well, maybe I am. Or I wouldn't be sitting here locked in my own handcuffs. But, I still can't figure it. What did you do with her gloves?"*

"Well goddamn, dumbass! I put 'em on and fired a shot with my left hand, so the powder burns'd be in the right place! Pretty smart, huh?"

"Yeah . . . It was. But how'd you get her to come to the bluff?"

"I just called her up and said I had some info about her brother, but I didn't want Bitsy to know we was talkin', that I didn't want her getting any more crazy than she already was . . . She was the one said where to meet, not me. I got there first on foot and hid on the ledge. It was really easier than I thought. She was so fuckin' sure of herself! When she reached down to help me up I blew her brains out. Then all I had to do was switch gloves, drop the pistol and leave."

"But what about Morgana? Why'd you kill her?"

"Same reason, you stupid turd. She came to my house asking about J.C. Offered me money if I'd tell her. Said she wanted to have his baby! After what my Coleeta went through on account of that boy and his loose prick . . . and now here was a goddamn queer wanting to have his baby for another queer! It was all I could do to wait till that night to finish her off."

There was a short buzzing on the tape, then muffled thumps and Collin's voice growled again. "This is it. Get out!"

The sound of the engine died away, then Bubba spoke. "What're you doing?"

"I'm fixin' to get rid of you, shithead. Whatta you think? And then I'm gonna get that old bag that keeps pryin' where she ain't wanted and stick her in here with you . . . Almost had 'er the other night. Woulda too, if the storm hadn't knocked out the *electricity. Couldn't believe my eyes when I saw that R.V. come crashin' outta that garage. Piece of bad luck, that was . . ."*

Collin's voice was jerky and breathless as he jammed the firebox full of wood.

"How come you tried to burn them up? And the business with the hot tub? Wouldn't just shooting them have been easier?"

Collin's voice hardened as he answered in a low hiss. *"No. It wasn't proper. All of you bastards have to burn in hell — just like me and Bitsy will."*

"But I still don't understan —" Bubba's voice was cut off as a sickening *crunch* sounded on the tape. Then Collin's voice again. *"You don't need to understand anything else, asshole. Ay-dee-ose!* Scraping noises came from the recording, then a hollow metallic *clunk,* and then just the echoing of muffled words as Collin continued to mumble while he set fire to the wood.

Bubba clicked off the recorder. He and the three women sat very still for a moment in the heavy silence of the hospital room.

Belle was the first to speak. "I'm so glad Poppy found you when she did. I'm so proud of her." She grasped Poppy's arm and smiled at her. "But it frightens me every time I think of how close we came to losing *both* of you."

Bubba looked embarrassed but pleased as Red patted him about mid-thigh, then leaned forward and kissed his cheek saying, "I'm glad she found you too, honey." She slid her hand up a little farther and grinned, "And I'm glad everything's still in working order."

"Beverly! Behave yourself." He batted away his

198

wife's roving fingers and chastely pulled the sheet up to his chest.

Red beamed at Poppy and Belle. "Delbert has some news for you, but I do too. And I get to tell mine first." She squared her shoulders and continued. "We've decided it's time to start our family."

Poppy suppressed a chuckle as she perceived a slight reactionary rise from the region of Bubba's sheeted lap. She spoke quickly to save the young deputy from further embarrassment. "Well, that's just great — big decision. Congratulations!" She paused, then went on. "I have some news of my own — Violet Cooper sends her best wishes and says to get with her, Red, on what to do with that mountain of Christmas presents she's bought for the kids and moms as the Women's Shelter. And she and Lupe are all fired up to start the live-in/work program at the ranch for the women at the shelter — especially for women with children."

Red nodded, grinning widely as Poppy went on. "She also says, Bubba, that she wants to give you a replacement for your Chevy that Drake dumped in the river. She says for you to pick it out and she'll send the bank draft to cover it."

Bubba began a sort of *oh-no-I-couldn't* movement with his hand but Red cut him off in mid-macho. "That's *wonderful*." She shot a flinty warning look at Bubba. "We are *very* grateful. The Suburban wasn't insured because Delbert used it for police work."

Poppy noticed the sheet over Bubba's lap had flattened out appreciably. *Ah, well. Betcha they work it out somehow.* She noted he now had a good grip on Red's hand.

"Hey, it's *my* turn now," Bubba said with a grin.

199

"I've been accepted as a technology instructor at the North Texas Police Academy down at Dallas. As soon as they let me out of this happy-jacket, we'll be moving down there." His grin widened and his eyes sparkled at the prospect, Poppy supposed, of all those gadgets and boy-toys he would finally have permission to indulge in.

Poppy leaned forward to shake his hand and was conscious of the weight of the Rojo County Sheriff's badge in her shirt pocket. "Oh yeah. I almost forgot." She finished the handshake, squeezing hard despite the painful response in her knuckles. She dug out the shiny star. "Here," she extended her hand. "I need to turn this in."

"Nope." Bubba shook his head. "You earned it . . . you keep it." He looked at Poppy, his eyes suddenly bright with moisture. "We might be doin' business again some time and I might not have time to swear you in."

"Thanks, son," Poppy answered, her own voice gruff with emotion. She wanted to say she appreciated it. That she and Belle wanted to be godparents of the child he and Red would soon make, and that they'd sure be happy to have the young couple visit them after Belle and Cleo got all moved into Poppy's little brick house at 5520 Mistletoe in Dallas. A house that probably wouldn't have a dog to greet them but . . .

But she didn't say any of that. She just swallowed past the lump in her throat and said again, "Thanks, son . . . thanks a lot."

A few of the publications of
THE NAIAD PRESS, INC.
P.O. Box 10543 ● Tallahassee, Florida 32302
Phone (904) 539-5965
Mail orders welcome. Please include 15% postage.

MURDER AT RED ROOK RANCH by Dorothy Tell. 224 pp.
First Poppy Dillworth adventure.   ISBN 0-941483-80-0 $8.95

LESBIAN SURVIVAL MANUAL by Rhonda Dicksion.
112 pp. Cartoons!   ISBN 0-941483-71-1   8.95

A ROOM FULL OF WOMEN by Elisabeth Nonas. 256 pp.
Contemporary Lesbian lives.   ISBN 0-941483-69-X   8.95

MURDER IS RELATIVE by Karen Saum. 256 pp. The first
Brigid Donovan mystery.   ISBN 0-941483-70-3   8.95

PRIORITIES by Lynda Lyons 288 pp. Science fiction with a
twist.   ISBN 0-941483-66-5   8.95

THEME FOR DIVERSE INSTRUMENTS by Jane Rule.
208 pp. Powerful romantic lesbian stories.   ISBN 0-941483-63-0   8.95

LESBIAN QUERIES by Hertz & Ertman. 112 pp. The questions
you were too embarrassed to ask.   ISBN 0-941483-67-3   8.95

CLUB 12 by Amanda Kyle Williams. 288 pp. Espionage thriller
featuring a lesbian agent!   ISBN 0-941483-64-9   8.95

DEATH DOWN UNDER by Claire McNab. 240 pp. 3rd Det.
Insp. Carol Ashton mystery.   ISBN 0-941483-39-8   8.95

MONTANA FEATHERS by Penny Hayes. 256 pp. Vivian and
Elizabeth find love in frontier Montana.   ISBN 0-941483-61-4   8.95

CHESAPEAKE PROJECT by Phyllis Horn. 304 pp. Jessie &
Meredith in perilous adventure.   ISBN 0-941483-58-4   8.95

LIFESTYLES by Jackie Calhoun. 224 pp. Contemporary Lesbian
lives and loves.   ISBN 0-941483-57-6   8.95

VIRAGO by Karen Marie Christa Minns. 208 pp. Darsen has
chosen Ginny.   ISBN 0-941483-56-8   8.95

WILDERNESS TREK by Dorothy Tell. 192 pp. Six women on
vacation learning "new" skills.   ISBN 0-941483-60-6   8.95

MURDER BY THE BOOK by Pat Welch. 256 pp. A Helen
Black Mystery. First in a series.   ISBN 0-941483-59-2   8.95

BERRIGAN by Vicki P. McConnell. 176 pp. Youthful Lesbian—
romantic, idealistic Berrigan.   ISBN 0-941483-55-X   8.95

LESBIANS IN GERMANY by Lillian Faderman & B. Eriksson.
128 pp. Fiction, poetry, essays.   ISBN 0-941483-62-2   8.95

THE BEVERLY MALIBU by Katherine V. Forrest. 288 pp. A
Kate Delafield Mystery. 3rd in a series.   ISBN 0-941483-47-9   16.95

THERE'S SOMETHING I'VE BEEN MEANING TO TELL
YOU Ed. by Loralee MacPike. 288 pp. Gay men and lesbians
coming out to their children.   ISBN 0-941483-44-4   9.95
      ISBN 0-941483-54-1   16.95

LIFTING BELLY by Gertrude Stein. Ed. by Rebecca Mark. 104
pp. Erotic poetry.   ISBN 0-941483-51-7   8.95
      ISBN 0-941483-53-3   14.95

ROSE PENSKI by Roz Perry. 192 pp. Adult lovers in a long-term
relationship.   ISBN 0-941483-37-1   8.95

AFTER THE FIRE by Jane Rule. 256 pp. Warm, human novel
by this incomparable author.   ISBN 0-941483-45-2   8.95

SUE SLATE, PRIVATE EYE by Lee Lynch. 176 pp. The gay
folk of Peacock Alley are *all* cats.   ISBN 0-941483-52-5   8.95

CHRIS by Randy Salem. 224 pp. Golden oldie. Handsome Chris
and her adventures.   ISBN 0-941483-42-8   8.95

THREE WOMEN by March Hastings. 232 pp. Golden oldie. A
triangle among wealthy sophisticates.   ISBN 0-941483-43-6   8.95

RICE AND BEANS by Valeria Taylor. 232 pp. Love and
romance on poverty row.   ISBN 0-941483-41-X   8.95

PLEASURES by Robbi Sommers. 204 pp. Unprecedented
eroticism.   ISBN 0-941483-49-5   8.95

EDGEWISE by Camarin Grae. 372 pp. Spellbinding
adventure.   ISBN 0-941483-19-3   9.95

FATAL REUNION by Claire McNab. 216 pp. 2nd Det. Inspec.
Carol Ashton mystery.   ISBN 0-941483-40-1   8.95

KEEP TO ME STRANGER by Sarah Aldridge. 372 pp. Romance
set in a department store dynasty.   ISBN 0-941483-38-X   9.95

HEARTSCAPE by Sue Gambill. 204 pp. American lesbian in
Portugal.   ISBN 0-941483-33-9   8.95

IN THE BLOOD by Lauren Wright Douglas. 252 pp. Lesbian
science fiction adventure fantasy   ISBN 0-941483-22-3   8.95

THE BEE'S KISS by Shirley Verel. 216 pp. Delicate, delicious
romance.   ISBN 0-941483-36-3   8.95

RAGING MOTHER MOUNTAIN by Pat Emmerson. 264 pp.
Furosa Firechild's adventures in Wonderland. ISBN 0-941483-35-5   8.95

IN EVERY PORT by Karin Kallmaker. 228 pp. Jessica's sexy,
adventuresome travels.   ISBN 0-941483-37-7   8.95

OF LOVE AND GLORY by Evelyn Kennedy. 192 pp. Exciting
WWII romance.   ISBN 0-941483-32-0   8.95

CLICKING STONES by Nancy Tyler Glenn. 288 pp. Love
transcending time.   ISBN 0-941483-31-2   8.95

SURVIVING SISTERS by Gail Pass. 252 pp. Powerful love
story.   ISBN 0-941483-16-9   8.95

SOUTH OF THE LINE by Catherine Ennis. 216 pp. Civil War
adventure.   ISBN 0-941483-29-0   8.95

WOMAN PLUS WOMAN by Dolores Klaich. 300 pp. Supurb
Lesbian overview.   ISBN 0-941483-28-2   9.95

SLOW DANCING AT MISS POLLY'S by Sheila Ortiz Taylor.
96 pp. Lesbian Poetry   ISBN 0-941483-30-4   7.95

DOUBLE DAUGHTER by Vicki P. McConnell. 216 pp. A Nyla
Wade Mystery, third in the series.   ISBN 0-941483-26-6   8.95

HEAVY GILT by Delores Klaich. 192 pp. Lesbian detective/
disappearing homophobes/upper class gay society.

                                               ISBN 0-941483-25-8   8.95

THE FINER GRAIN by Denise Ohio. 216 pp. Brilliant young
college lesbian novel.   ISBN 0-941483-11-8   8.95

THE AMAZON TRAIL by Lee Lynch. 216 pp. Life, travel & lore
of famous lesbian author.   ISBN 0-941483-27-4   8.95

HIGH CONTRAST by Jessie Lattimore. 264 pp. Women of the
Crystal Palace.   ISBN 0-941483-17-7   8.95

OCTOBER OBSESSION by Meredith More. Josie's rich, secret
Lesbian life.   ISBN 0-941483-18-5   8.95

LESBIAN CROSSROADS by Ruth Baetz. 276 pp. Contemporary
Lesbian lives.   ISBN 0-941483-21-5   9.95

BEFORE STONEWALL: THE MAKING OF A GAY AND
LESBIAN COMMUNITY by Andrea Weiss & Greta Schiller.
96 pp., 25 illus.   ISBN 0-941483-20-7   7.95

WE WALK THE BACK OF THE TIGER by Patricia A. Murphy.
192 pp. Romantic Lesbian novel/beginning women's movement.

                                               ISBN 0-941483-13-4   8.95

SUNDAY'S CHILD by Joyce Bright. 216 pp. Lesbian athletics, at
last the novel about sports.   ISBN 0-941483-12-6   8.95

OSTEN'S BAY by Zenobia N. Vole. 204 pp. Sizzling adventure
romance set on Bonaire.   ISBN 0-941483-15-0   8.95

LESSONS IN MURDER by Claire McNab. 216 pp. 1st Det. Inspec.
Carol Ashton mystery — erotic tension!.   ISBN 0-941483-14-2   8.95

YELLOWTHROAT by Penny Hayes. 240 pp. Margarita, bandit,
kidnaps Julia.   ISBN 0-941483-10-X   8.95

SAPPHISTRY: THE BOOK OF LESBIAN SEXUALITY by
Pat Califia. 3d edition, revised. 208 pp.   ISBN 0-941483-24-X   8.95

CHERISHED LOVE by Evelyn Kennedy. 192 pp. Erotic
Lesbian love story.   ISBN 0-941483-08-8   8.95

LAST SEPTEMBER by Helen R. Hull. 208 pp. Six stories & a glorious novella. ISBN 0-941483-09-6   8.95

THE SECRET IN THE BIRD by Camarin Grae. 312 pp. Striking, psychological suspense novel. ISBN 0-941483-05-3   8.95

TO THE LIGHTNING by Catherine Ennis. 208 pp. Romantic Lesbian 'Robinson Crusoe' adventure. ISBN 0-941483-06-1   8.95

THE OTHER SIDE OF VENUS by Shirley Verel. 224 pp. Luminous, romantic love story. ISBN 0-941483-07-X   8.95

DREAMS AND SWORDS by Katherine V. Forrest. 192 pp. Romantic, erotic, imaginative stories. ISBN 0-941483-03-7   8.95

MEMORY BOARD by Jane Rule. 336 pp. Memorable novel about an aging Lesbian couple. ISBN 0-941483-02-9   9.95

THE ALWAYS ANONYMOUS BEAST by Lauren Wright Douglas. 224 pp. A Caitlin Reese mystery. First in a series. ISBN 0-941483-04-5   8.95

SEARCHING FOR SPRING by Patricia A. Murphy. 224 pp. Novel about the recovery of love. ISBN 0-941483-00-2   8.95

DUSTY'S QUEEN OF HEARTS DINER by Lee Lynch. 240 pp. Romantic blue-collar novel. ISBN 0-941483-01-0   8.95

PARENTS MATTER by Ann Muller. 240 pp. Parents' relationships with Lesbian daughters and gay sons. ISBN 0-930044-91-6   9.95

THE PEARLS by Shelley Smith. 176 pp. Passion and fun in the Caribbean sun. ISBN 0-930044-93-2   7.95

MAGDALENA by Sarah Aldridge. 352 pp. Epic Lesbian novel set on three continents. ISBN 0-930044-99-1   8.95

THE BLACK AND WHITE OF IT by Ann Allen Shockley. 144 pp. Short stories. ISBN 0-930044-96-7   7.95

SAY JESUS AND COME TO ME by Ann Allen Shockley. 288 pp. Contemporary romance. ISBN 0-930044-98-3   8.95

LOVING HER by Ann Allen Shockley. 192 pp. Romantic love story. ISBN 0-930044-97-5   7.95

MURDER AT THE NIGHTWOOD BAR by Katherine V. Forrest. 240 pp. A Kate Delafield mystery. Second in a series. ISBN 0-930044-92-4   8.95

ZOE'S BOOK by Gail Pass. 224 pp. Passionate, obsessive love story. ISBN 0-930044-95-9   7.95

WINGED DANCER by Camarin Grae. 228 pp. Erotic Lesbian adventure story. ISBN 0-930044-88-6   8.95

PAZ by Camarin Grae. 336 pp. Romantic Lesbian adventurer with the power to change the world. ISBN 0-930044-89-4   8.95

SOUL SNATCHER by Camarin Grae. 224 pp. A puzzle, an
adventure, a mystery — Lesbian romance.   ISBN 0-930044-90-8   8.95

THE LOVE OF GOOD WOMEN by Isabel Miller. 224 pp.
Long-awaited new novel by the author of the beloved *Patience
and Sarah*.   ISBN 0-930044-81-9   8.95

THE HOUSE AT PELHAM FALLS by Brenda Weathers. 240
pp. Suspenseful Lesbian ghost story.   ISBN 0-930044-79-7   7.95

HOME IN YOUR HANDS by Lee Lynch. 240 pp. More stories
from the author of *Old Dyke Tales*.   ISBN 0-930044-80-0   7.95

EACH HAND A MAP by Anita Skeen. 112 pp. Real-life poems
that touch us all.   ISBN 0-930044-82-7   6.95

SURPLUS by Sylvia Stevenson. 342 pp. A classic early Lesbian
novel.   ISBN 0-930044-78-9   7.95

PEMBROKE PARK by Michelle Martin. 256 pp. Derring-do
and daring romance in Regency England.   ISBN 0-930044-77-0   7.95

THE LONG TRAIL by Penny Hayes. 248 pp. Vivid adventures
of two women in love in the old west.   ISBN 0-930044-76-2   8.95

HORIZON OF THE HEART by Shelley Smith. 192 pp. Hot
romance in summertime New England.   ISBN 0-930044-75-4   7.95

AN EMERGENCE OF GREEN by Katherine V. Forrest. 288
pp. Powerful novel of sexual discovery.   ISBN 0-930044-69-X   8.95

THE LESBIAN PERIODICALS INDEX edited by Claire
Potter. 432 pp. Author & subject index.   ISBN 0-930044-74-6   29.95

DESERT OF THE HEART by Jane Rule. 224 pp. A classic;
basis for the movie *Desert Hearts*.   ISBN 0-930044-73-8   8.95

SPRING FORWARD/FALL BACK by Sheila Ortiz Taylor.
288 pp. Literary novel of timeless love.   ISBN 0-930044-70-3   7.95

FOR KEEPS by Elisabeth Nonas. 144 pp. Contemporary novel
about losing and finding love.   ISBN 0-930044-71-1   7.95

TORCHLIGHT TO VALHALLA by Gale Wilhelm. 128 pp.
Classic novel by a great Lesbian writer.   ISBN 0-930044-68-1   7.95

LESBIAN NUNS: BREAKING SILENCE edited by Rosemary
Curb and Nancy Manahan. 432 pp. Unprecedented autobiographies
of religious life.   ISBN 0-930044-62-2   9.95

THE SWASHBUCKLER by Lee Lynch. 288 pp. Colorful novel
set in Greenwich Village in the sixties.   ISBN 0-930044-66-5   8.95

MISFORTUNE'S FRIEND by Sarah Aldridge. 320 pp. Histori-
cal Lesbian novel set on two continents.   ISBN 0-930044-67-3   7.95

A STUDIO OF ONE'S OWN by Ann Stokes. Edited by
Dolores Klaich. 128 pp. Autobiography.   ISBN 0-930044-64-9   7.95

SEX VARIANT WOMEN IN LITERATURE by Jeannette
Howard Foster. 448 pp. Literary history.   ISBN 0-930044-65-7   8.95

A HOT-EYED MODERATE by Jane Rule. 252 pp. Hard-hitting essays on gay life; writing; art. ISBN 0-930044-57-6 — 7.95

INLAND PASSAGE AND OTHER STORIES by Jane Rule. 288 pp. Wide-ranging new collection. ISBN 0-930044-56-8 — 7.95

WE TOO ARE DRIFTING by Gale Wilhelm. 128 pp. Timeless Lesbian novel, a masterpiece. ISBN 0-930044-61-4 — 6.95

AMATEUR CITY by Katherine V. Forrest. 224 pp. A Kate Delafield mystery. First in a series. ISBN 0-930044-55-X — 8.95

THE SOPHIE HOROWITZ STORY by Sarah Schulman. 176 pp. Engaging novel of madcap intrigue. ISBN 0-930044-54-1 — 7.95

THE BURNTON WIDOWS by Vickie P. McConnell. 272 pp. A Nyla Wade mystery, second in the series. ISBN 0-930044-52-5 — 7.95

OLD DYKE TALES by Lee Lynch. 224 pp. Extraordinary stories of our diverse Lesbian lives. ISBN 0-930044-51-7 — 8.95

DAUGHTERS OF A CORAL DAWN by Katherine V. Forrest. 240 pp. Novel set in a Lesbian new world. ISBN 0-930044-50-9 — 8.95

THE PRICE OF SALT by Claire Morgan. 288 pp. A milestone novel, a beloved classic. ISBN 0-930044-49-5 — 8.95

AGAINST THE SEASON by Jane Rule. 224 pp. Luminous, complex novel of interrelationships. ISBN 0-930044-48-7 — 8.95

LOVERS IN THE PRESENT AFTERNOON by Kathleen Fleming. 288 pp. A novel about recovery and growth. ISBN 0-930044-46-0 — 8.95

TOOTHPICK HOUSE by Lee Lynch. 264 pp. Love between two Lesbians of different classes. ISBN 0-930044-45-2 — 7.95

MADAME AURORA by Sarah Aldridge. 256 pp. Historical novel featuring a charismatic "seer." ISBN 0-930044-44-4 — 7.95

CURIOUS WINE by Katherine V. Forrest. 176 pp. Passionate Lesbian love story, a best-seller. ISBN 0-930044-43-6 — 8.95

BLACK LESBIAN IN WHITE AMERICA by Anita Cornwell. 141 pp. Stories, essays, autobiography. ISBN 0-930044-41-X — 7.95

CONTRACT WITH THE WORLD by Jane Rule. 340 pp. Powerful, panoramic novel of gay life. ISBN 0-930044-28-2 — 9.95

MRS. PORTER'S LETTER by Vicki P. McConnell. 224 pp. The first Nyla Wade mystery. ISBN 0-930044-29-0 — 7.95

TO THE CLEVELAND STATION by Carol Anne Douglas. 192 pp. Interracial Lesbian love story. ISBN 0-930044-27-4 — 6.95

THE NESTING PLACE by Sarah Aldridge. 224 pp. A three-woman triangle—love conquers all! ISBN 0-930044-26-6 — 7.95

THIS IS NOT FOR YOU by Jane Rule. 284 pp. A letter to a beloved is also an intricate novel. ISBN 0-930044-25-8 — 8.95

FAULTLINE by Sheila Ortiz Taylor. 140 pp. Warm, funny, literate story of a startling family. ISBN 0-930044-24-X 6.95

THE LESBIAN IN LITERATURE by Barbara Grier. 3d ed. Foreword by Maida Tilchen. 240 pp. Comprehensive bibliography. Literary ratings; rare photos. ISBN 0-930044-23-1 7.95

ANNA'S COUNTRY by Elizabeth Lang. 208 pp. A woman finds her Lesbian identity. ISBN 0-930044-19-3 6.95

PRISM by Valerie Taylor. 158 pp. A love affair between two women in their sixties. ISBN 0-930044-18-5 6.95

BLACK LESBIANS: AN ANNOTATED BIBLIOGRAPHY compiled by J. R. Roberts. Foreword by Barbara Smith. 112 pp. Award-winning bibliography. ISBN 0-930044-21-5 5.95

THE MARQUISE AND THE NOVICE by Victoria Ramstetter. 108 pp. A Lesbian Gothic novel. ISBN 0-930044-16-9 6.95

OUTLANDER by Jane Rule. 207 pp. Short stories and essays by one of our finest writers. ISBN 0-930044-17-7 8.95

ALL TRUE LOVERS by Sarah Aldridge. 292 pp. Romantic novel set in the 1930s and 1940s. ISBN 0-930044-10-X 7.95

A WOMAN APPEARED TO ME by Renee Vivien. 65 pp. A classic; translated by Jeannette H. Foster. ISBN 0-930044-06-1 5.00

CYTHEREA'S BREATH by Sarah Aldridge. 240 pp. Romantic novel about women's entrance into medicine.
ISBN 0-930044-02-9 6.95

TOTTIE by Sarah Aldridge. 181 pp. Lesbian romance in the turmoil of the sixties. ISBN 0-930044-01-0 6.95

THE LATECOMER by Sarah Aldridge. 107 pp. A delicate love story. ISBN 0-930044-00-2 6.95

ODD GIRL OUT by Ann Bannon. ISBN 0-930044-83-5 5.95

I AM A WOMAN by Ann Bannon. ISBN 0-930044-84-3 5.95

WOMEN IN THE SHADOWS by Ann Bannon.
ISBN 0-930044-85-1 5.95

JOURNEY TO A WOMAN by Ann Bannon.
ISBN 0-930044-86-X 5.95

BEEBO BRINKER by Ann Bannon. ISBN 0-930044-87-8 5.95
Legendary novels written in the fifties and sixties, set in the gay mecca of Greenwich Village.

VOLUTE BOOKS

JOURNEY TO FULFILLMENT	Early classics by Valerie	3.95
A WORLD WITHOUT MEN	Taylor: The Erika Frohmann	3.95
RETURN TO LESBOS	series.	3.95

These are just a few of the many Naiad Press titles — we are the oldest and largest lesbian/feminist publishing company in the world. Please request a complete catalog. We offer personal service; we encourage and welcome direct mail orders from individuals who have limited access to bookstores carrying our publications.